FLAPPING MY LEFT WING

Hannah Ruth Price

"The sky is falling!"

— CHICKEN LITTLE

"What is life but one long risk?"

— DOROTHY CANFIELD FISHER

"A fish may love a bird, but where would they live?"

— DREW BARRYMORE

"If one sticks too rigidly to one's principles, one would hardly see anybody."

— AGATHA CHRISTIE

"I did not become a vegetarian for my health. I did it for the health of the chickens."

— ISAAC BASHEVIS SINGER

To Sam and Jess

The Bad Dream

Awakened by the call of nature in the wee hours of early morning, Ms. Little, affectionately known to her pals as Chick, padded bleary-eyed to the bathroom, and stepped in WATER!! Nearly an inch of it, right up to her cute little ankles.

"Awk!" cried Chick. "What the devil is going on?" Simultaneously, as she flicked the switch for the hall light, a light came on in Chick's head.

"The ICE is melting! The ICE is melting! I must tell the King!" squawked Chick, and, rushing out the door, still clad in her flannel nightie (the one with the holes in it) she jumped in her SUV, wings akimbo, feathers flying, and sped off.

Oh, my, she thought suddenly. I'd better stop at Henny Penny's and warn her. And so, making a quick detour, she pulled up smartly in front of her friend's new condo, blasting the horn in spite of ordinances. But Henny blew her off, saying she was too busy, on her way to a big sale at the mall, and to just call her later.

Perplexed at her friend's insensitivity and lack of compassion for the fate of the planet, nonetheless, our intrepid harbinger of bad news carried on, remembering with a start that Henny was a Republican.

None too soon, she arrived at the White House and asked breathlessly for an audience with King George, the newly crowned Emperor. He had issued an open door policy since re-writing the Constitution and all were invited to plead their cause. Tapping her foot for a good two hours while common folk begged for all manner of frivolity, like heating oil and health insurance, which, while important, were simply not an emergency like her own Big News, thought Chick.

Finally it was Miss Little's turn. She bowed gracefully, under pressure to come across as believable while wearing her nightgown, breath that could bowl you over, and, she realized with chagrin, bedhead.

Unflappable, Chick stepped up to the Golden Throne. "Sir!" she said in her strongest voice. "I have news! The ICE is melting! Remember Al Gore? The man that actually won the . . ." Chick stopped herself just in time. "Mr. Gore? He was right. The Earth is warming and the ICE is melting! Look! I have proof."

Ms. Little held up her foot, which was by now, bone-dry.

"I think maybe I heared this story somewhere before, not precisely, positively, absolutely," said the King with a frown on his face. "But looky here, I'm the Decider and I say the Earth will not be warming! Hogwash. Quit pestering me. Be off with you or I'll have your head."

With that, Ms. Little ran away just as fast as her stubby little legs could carry her. She knew all too well about heads being chopped off, many of her contemporaries having met that very fate.

"Shit!" said Ms. Little, in a rare burst of profanity. "No

one will listen to me. I'm going to have lunch at McBlat-Burger's, go shopping, buy a flat screen TV, and shut up."

Shortly, there she was at the mall, about to bite into a Big Blat, when POOF! . . . Chick woke up, sweating profusely, all twisted up in her sheets, but safe in her own little bed.

"Why, I was having a nightmare!" exclaimed Chick out loud. "George Bush is still the President, but thank goodness, he's not the King. And I wouldn't be caught dead driving a gas guzzling SUV. I don't even drive. Certainly the only reason I'd ever enter a McBlatBurger is to use their facilities."

Chick climbed out of bed to get a drink of water and thankfully found the floor nice and dry. She had seen Gore's movie, *An Inconvenient Truth*, the minute it came out, and had worked alongside other local activists promoting solutions to what Chick felt was the biggest crisis the planet Earth and all her inhabitants had ever faced. Increasingly frustrated at the lack of progress and the lack of any meaningful change on the part of just about everyone, she had lately realized she was downright burnt out.

What was a chicken to do?

"You know, that's not a bad idea," said Chick out loud. "I'll go to the mall, buy myself some new clothes, a nice comfy recliner, and a great big TV."

And that's exactly what she did.

2

The Burning Question

A few short months ago, our heroine, Chick Little, had tuned in and dropped out, pledging to spend her time shopping and vegging out in front of her new flat screen TV, watching Survivor reruns. But doggone, if she didn't find herself on Monday at 5:00 p.m., trudging down to the crossroads of her little village to stand with a handful of other women holding peace signs. These women and an occasional man had been on the corner every week for over six months, protesting the war in Iraq, in support of the troops, but calling for an end to the occupation and bringing them home. And impeach Bush and Cheney, to boot. To stand with them was the least Chick felt she could do. She was warmly welcomed even though she was so short she could barely be seen.

At least I'm doing something, the chicken said to herself as she held up her 'Honk For Peace' sign. She appreciated the camaraderie, especially since she and her closest friend, Henny Penny, had drifted apart. Henny had voted for John McCain in the primary and Chick could hardly contain her disappointment. She herself was a staunch supporter of Hillary Clinton. It was high time a woman was in charge of the USA. Forty-three men were more than enough. But Chick was worried. If the women in Texas and Ohio didn't come through with a strong Democratic showing on March 4th, the nominee would be Barack Obama. Let him be VP, Chick fumed. She considered herself a feminist and though she'd been married twice, had kept her maiden name, to use an antiquated phrase. Quite unfortunately that name was Sanders. For if there was anyone she came close to hating, it was Colonel Sanders. Yes, she thought with a glimpse of introspection, I do hold hate in my heart. Colonel Sanders, George Bush, Dick Cheney. Bad men. And the list of dictators published in last Sunday's paper, Kim Jong-ii, King Abdullah, Robert Mugabe, Ali Khamenei. More men. Extremely bad men.

This was the burning question that kept Chicklet's eyes wide open at night, haunted her dreams, and found her on the computer at 2:00 a.m. What is the root cause of the propensity for violence in the male of the human species and how can these violent tendencies be subjugated? She had her theories, but unfortunately, no viable solutions. As she perused the daily online headlines, it was only too obvious that it was open season on women. It was open season on chickens, too, sadly enough, and Chick felt there was a correlation. A lifelong vegetarian and now a vegan, she was appalled at the insensitivity of humanity to other species. Peace begins in the kitchen, she believed.

Oh, if only everyone had the heart of Gandhi, sighed Chick. Now there was a real man. A good man. Try as she would, she fell far short of her aspirations to follow in his footsteps. Chick knew her own little four-toed carbon footprint was relatively dainty and left barely a mark. She didn't own a car. She'd never even used a clothes dryer, for heaven's sake. Was Gandhi a Buddhist? She chastised herself for her ignorance on this point. A quick search on the internet told her he was a Sanatani Hindu. Although she looked upon organized religion with disdain, finding it overwhelmingly hypocritical, Chick was drawn to Buddhism. She'd spent an enlightening weekend only last year at a Kadampa meditation center, joining other like-minded souls in a loving kindness compassion retreat. Chick found it easy to feel empathy for those she loved, much more difficult to extend benevolent thoughts toward her enemies. Struggling to pronounce Arya Avalokiteshvara, a bodhisattva who contains the compassion of all Buddhas, she found it to be a real tongue twister for a chicken. Many lessons lay ahead of her, pronunciation being the least of them.

Deep in contemplation of her own Buddha nature while standing on the street corner, Chick felt in tune with the oneness of all life and could clearly see her own role as a mere player on a stage. All these thoughts and more went through her mind as she stood holding her sign, which had become quite heavy during the last hour. As the demonstrators walked to their cars, the group made plans to go for a pizza after their stand next week, kindly including Chick.

"As long as it's vegan, I'd love to," she said, smiling with gratitude at her new friends.

As the weekend rolled around, she received a reminder for Standing Up For Peace and felt herself becoming energized. Thank goodness, I think I've rediscovered my social conscience, thought Chick. Maybe I could round up a few friends to join the group. She knew that inviting Henny was a lost cause, but perhaps Turkey Lurkey and Goosey Loosey would accompany her. Ducky Lucky was off skiing in North Carolina, the lucky dog.

"Hi Turk, it's me," said Chick when Turkey answered the phone.

"Me . . . I know quite a number of folks named me, including me," Turkey said in a vaguely sarcastic tone.

"Oh, Turkey, cut the crap. I have something important to tell you," replied Chick, already exasperated.

"You always do, my dear Chick. I believe last time it was something about the sky?"

"That was a long time ago, Turkey." Chick's face turned hot with embarrassment as she recalled the acorn incident. Still, Chick told him with enthusiasm, all about her stand on the corner last week and the inspiring women she'd met.

"Oh, Chick, Chick, Chick," Turkey gave a long drawn out sigh. "When will you learn? The sixties are over. Everything is done on the internet these days. Yes, I fully support your efforts but I shall be protesting from the comfort of my armchair, thank you very much. Count me out, honey. But give Goosey a jingle. She may well be up for making a public display of herself. I hear she's lost fifteen pounds," chortled Turkey. "Ta-tata. Gotta go. Ciao."

Geez, men, thought Chick. Why do I bother? She dialed Goosey, who was delighted to hear from her until Chick asked her to stand on the corner protesting the war.

"Oh, dear. I just couldn't. Not here in town. You know I'm a realtor and I have to be careful of what I do. I could lose clients. I'm so sorry. I'll go to DC with you or Orlando again, but I can't be controversial in our little village. Try Ducky or Henny Penny," said her friend.

"Ducky's out of town . . . and Henny . . . well, she's not the Henny we knew anymore. She told me she's voting for McCain."

"Honk! What?" yelled Goosey, coughing and choking on the slice of chocolate cake she was enjoying as they spoke. "You must be joking."

"I wish I were. She told me she switched her party from Green to Republican. I simply cannot believe she's not backing Hillary."

"Oh, that can't be true," said Goosey, calming down a bit. "No woman in her right mind would vote for that

7

man. And he may choose Huckabee as his running mate. I swear if those two end up in the White House, I'm heading to Mexico."

Chick was beginning to feel uneasy about Henny. Was there something amiss with her old friend's mind? Surely no woman in full possession of her faculties would support a man like John McCain, a man who would keep our country in Iraq for . . . how long? A hundred years? A thousand years? A man who was quite happy to have the support of Pastor John Hagee, a televangelist worth millions that Chick had nightmares about. Yes, McCain was Bush with a brain, a clever and calculating brain.

Something was definitely going on with Henny, mused Chick. She'd been dressing strangely of late, showing up at a Sierra Club meeting wearing a poodle skirt and red Converse high tops, forgetting that she too, sported the same footwear. Lost in this quite unpleasant reverie, she realized that Goosey was still on the phone, still chattering away.

"Sorry," said Chick. "I was spacing out. Let's do lunch soon. We'll go down to the Cup and Saucer. If Henny pulls that McCain ca-ca in there, she'll have to deal with Suzanne. Oh, by the way, I hear your new diet's working out."

"Uh, well . . . I had company, we ate out a lot, and you know, well, it's hard," stammered Goosey, her mouth still full of cake. "Call me. We'll meet up next Wednesday for music."

So, a bit disillusioned but still determined, Chick went to the corner on Monday without her closest friends. Sadly, this week only two other women showed up. A pickup truck slowed down as the passenger threw a handful of rotting fruit at the demonstrators.

"Get a job, hippie!" A young man leaned out of a car, his middle finger extended. I worked hard all my life, thought

Chick, as she wiped the dripping mango off her beak. Why can't we stop fighting and live in peace?

"Damn it all!" said Chick in an explosion of profanity that for her was becoming increasingly common. "Why aren't there hundreds of people out here protesting this illegal war?" Chick asked the others. And Goosey should be here. That would give new meaning to their sign, 'Honk For Peace'.

At least Chick still had her sense of humor.

3

The Elusive Idea

Chick knew she had a Good Idea. Alas, she had this idea in the middle of the night, in the throes of another bout with persistent insomnia, and now, in the clear light of early morning, she simply could not wrap her brain around that most brilliant idea. It had to do with peace, world peace, something I could do to promote world peace, Chick contemplated, as she lay in her bed wiggling her newly polished toes, listening to the welcome gurgling of the coffee pot. I could bicycle . . . no, not that . . . not swim, either . . . oh, yes, I could go on a peace walk to Tallahassee or even Washington DC. She had read with admiration of a young couple who had bicycled across the country last summer promoting a peaceful alternative to war, hoping to get folks thinking and talking about the war in Iraq.

"I could do this!" said Chick out loud, already excited about the possibility. But could I do it alone? If I can't even convince my friends to stand on the corner with me, undoubtedly they would not be up for a walk to Washington. Maybe one of the women from the Monday group would be interested, she thought, although they all seem to lead full lives, and had a staunch commitment to the weekly stand. And the logistics were problematic. I'd have to eat in a restaurant at least once a day and where would I stay? I couldn't count on a church every night and that would mean motels. And how would people know I was walking for peace? I guess I could wear a sign, like the old sandwich boards . . .

Chick gasped. How could I have come up with that analogy? On a sandwich board, would of course be . . . a chicken sandwich! Yes, there was a very real danger that someone would see her as . . . just a meal. The road could be a scary place for a woman alone, and infinitely worse for a small chicken. Her Good Idea was beginning to sound not quite as good. Looking at the situation realistically, could she really afford a trip like this? She had a modest nest egg, and though she could scarcely believe it, this year had reached the age of eligibility to collect Social Security. The Catch-22 here was . . . how long would she live? Her savings might possibly last her lifetime, barring unforeseen medical catastrophes. But what if she should live on? And on? Become a burden on her family? On society? One of life's little jokes, she said to herself. Put something away for a rainy day, they tell you. Yes, it's a rainy day, you run out to bring the clothes in from the line and lightning strikes you dead two weeks after you've retired. This actually happened to a high school acquaintance and ever since, Chick had checked the sky frequently when bringing in the laundry. All your scrimping and saving was possibly for naught. You only live once, thought Chick, although since her study of Buddhism she was no longer convinced of that concept.

I'm not going to spend my golden years worrying myself to death over money, she told herself. Okay, I can swing it financially, she decided. But was this walk really such a good idea after all? Chick pictured her rather tiny feet drudging step after step, mile after mile.

"I need coffee!" exclaimed Chick to Winnie, her stuffed rabbit. As she jumped out of bed she felt a familiar twinge of pain in her lower back. Oh, brilliant, she thought. I'll walk to Tallahassee. I'm so out of shape I get winded walking to the corner. I'm going to start that new exercise program today, she promised herself for the zillionth time.

The chicken settled on her porch with her mug of coffee, slowly sipping the life-giving fluid. If only I could drive, I could buy a van and put peace signs all over it and even sleep in it. Or I could make an Art Car. Or any one of a number of wonderful things!

Her inability to obtain a driver's license was one of the biggest personal frustrations of our little chicken's life. Goosey is so lucky, fumed Chick, briefly consumed with jealousy toward her dear friend. Goosey was just a foot and a half taller than Chick (depending on whose foot you used) but because of her added height, the goose could drive. Goosey had her own bright red MINI-Cooper, outfitted with special controls, and she could damn well go wherever she pleased, even though she mostly went shopping. But Chick was just too small. She couldn't go on certain rides at Disney World (she longed to ride Space Mountain) and she couldn't drive a car.

Suddenly a light bulb, the spirally kind, went off in Chick's head. The bus. I'll take the Greyhound Bus! Now that was a Good Idea. A tremendously Good Idea. I'll wear Code Pink tee shirts and all sorts of peace buttons and I'll pass out literature and talk to everyone, real people from all walks of life, and I'll start a blog so people can follow my progress and when I come back, I'll write a book and be on talk shows and NPR and I . . . I'll discover the heartbeat of America!

Chick grabbed her phone and punched in Goosey's

number. She couldn't wait to tell the goose and Henny Penny, too. But wait she would have to, since both their phones went straight to voicemail. In fact, she couldn't get hold of anyone at all and their favorite hangout had already closed. Frustrated, she was forced to leave a message.

"Meet me tomorrow at the Cup and Saucer, 10:30 a.m. sharp!" screeched Chick excitedly into the phone. "I have the most wonderful new Good Idea." She had no doubt her friends would be there.

The next morning brought its own challenges. She'd forgotten to arrange a ride to town and had to beg a neighbor to drive her in. I'm not always late, she thought, pushing open the door to the coffee shop at nearly 11:00 a.m.

"Chick!" Suzanne greeted her warmly as usual which she greatly appreciated. The place was jammed with the regulars, Dorito, Happy, Cookie. Even Turkey was there today, although it was Tuesday. He usually only made an appearance for Joni and her twangy ballads of West Virginia. Just as she had thought, there was Goosey and Henny, already enjoying a homemade quiche and a whole wheat bagel. Chick had to forgo the quiche. Eating an egg made her feel like a cannibal, although it didn't seem to bother her friends in the least.

"I'll just have a cup of your delicious coffee, please, Suzanne." Chick plunked herself down next to Goosey.

"Hey, girlfriend, now let's hear this great idea of yours." Goosey always got right to the point. "I'll have you know I rescheduled a house showing to meet you."

"You're so sweet. You look wonderful, Goosey," Chick said, giving her friend a big hug.

"I lost ten pounds and I'm going to lose ten more. I feel fantastic," said Goosey, barely remembering her chocolate indulgences of a few days ago.

"Okay, here's my idea," began Chick, and with great enthusiasm and many wing gestures, she excitedly outlined the details of her Great Greyhound Bus Adventure. "And I can get a 60-day Discovery Pass for $538. I'm hoping some of you will come with me," she finished up on a note of expectation.

There was a stunned silence. Finally Dorito, one of the women from the corner stand for peace, said quietly, "Well, that is quite an idea, Chick."

"Ride a bus? For two months? Oh, I don't know . . . I don't think . . . umm . . . I mean." For once, Goosey was speechless.

Suzanne spoke up. "I, for one, think it's a wonderful idea, Chick. A life-affirming journey for peace, an empowering step for your species and for women everywhere. I would go with you if I weren't stuck in this coffee shop, which, don't get me wrong, most days I dearly love."

"I'll go with you, Chick. It sounds like fun!" shouted Henny, just as her phone rang with annoying musical tones. She rushed outside out of respect for the others, and the big sign on the wall. 'No Cell Phones'.

"I only rode a Greyhound once in my life," said Happy with a faraway look on her face. Everyone began talking at once, weighing the pros and cons of Chick's Great Idea. Then Turkey, who had remained silent up until now, cleared his long throat loudly and stood up.

"Chick, do you have any grip on reality at all? You apparently are under a delusion that bus riders are a representative sampling of society. No, far from it, my dear, you will be dealing with the poor, the downtrodden, the alcoholic, the desperate fringe element, not to mention homeless veterans who may very well not only disagree with you, but wish you ill will. You will be seen as a dilettante, traveling by bus as a lark, while for your fellow riders, this mode of transportation may be the only one open to them. Believe me, you will not be welcomed with open arms, you and your message of peace. The true believers of God, guns, guts and country are out there in droves. Go down to the Deli right here in Two-Lip. You're naive, my dear Chick. You could well end up in a stew pot, along with dumplings and gravy. Just looking out for your well-being, sweetie." Giving Chick a pat on the head, he walked out the door.

"Humpf!" said Cookie. "Don't let the door hit you on your big fat feathered butt on your way out."

"What happened? Did I miss something?" queried Henny, coming back inside after her phone chat.

"A man was just giving his much overrated opinion," said Suzanne, rolling her eyes.

"His opinion on what?" asked Henny.

"My Greyhound bus trip for peace. Would you really go with me, Henny?" Chick was hoping for support, yet unsure as to how a Republican McCain supporter could be a rider for peace.

"Go on a bus? Why, I wouldn't be caught dead on a bus, those smelly dirty things, packed in like sardines with all manner of unpleasant characters, stopping at McBlat-Burger's to eat. Not me!" Henny threw up her wings dramatically.

"But Henny, you just told me twenty minutes ago that you'd go with me. That it would be fun," stammered Chick, puzzled.

"I most certainly did not. I would never even consider such a trip." Henny grabbed a tambourine and began dancing around the floor. Chick caught Goosey's eye. They were both thinking the same thing. There was something wrong with Henny.

Dorito said gently, "Doesn't your daughter live in Sarasota, Chick? Why not take the bus down to visit her? It would give you a chance to check it out before jumping in with both feet."

Chick looked at her gratefully. "You're right, Dorito. Thanks for thinking of that. I will. I'll do it soon."

4

A Different Trip

Chick gazed at her reflection in the bathroom mirror. Yes, she could almost see disillusionment written all over her face. Yesterday she'd been flying high, convinced her bus odyssey for peace was a Good Idea. BOOM! In one fell swoop, all her big plans came crashing to a halt, and with them her spirits.

I feel like going back to bed and staying there, thought Chick morosely. Maybe I am bipolar. In the early morning hours after another insomniac night, Chick had come to the realization that Turkey, bless his heart, had been right.

Last evening her friend, Dorito, had driven her to the Gainesville bus station to buy a ticket to Sarasota. Even though the sign said 'OPEN', the door was locked tight. The station was closed. A light drizzle had turned to rain as a small knot of people huddled against the wall, trying in vain to avoid the downpour. There were two women with small crying children, a forlorn looking man carrying what looked to be all his worldly goods, a huge scary guy with long greasy hair and a lot of tattoos, an extremely thin woman with hollow eyes. Everyone looked like they had problems, big ones. Her heart sank as Chick realized she couldn't go through with her plan. She couldn't go waltzing up in all her feathered finery, chattering about war protests and writing to your Senator to people who, in all probability, were wondering how to pay the rent, where their next meal was coming from, or where they would sleep tonight.

"I'm too chicken," she said to Dorito, so distracted she didn't even realize how absurd that sounded. This had not been a Good Idea after all. I'll have to think of something else, something meaningful, something Big. This refrain ran through her mind for the hundredth time. The reality was that she already spent a considerable amount of energy engaged in political activism of late, indeed for most of her life, small things to be sure, but every action helps one's cause. A friend had even given her a button that proclaimed, 'I'm Here To Save The Planet', which she wore frequently along with her 'Jail Bush' button.

Back home, she was about to turn on her TV and watch Dr. Phil when she remembered reading that he makes ninety-five million dollars a year. What does he do with all that money? And Bill Gates? The Waltons? Billionaires. The gap between the uber rich and the rest of us is a bottomless chasm. Chick felt the beginnings of a migraine, although she'd never had one. All this thinking was enough to give anyone a headache.

Getting up off the couch, she went into the bathroom intending to take a hot shower. Chick peered into the bathroom mirror again, inspecting a suspicious spot on her beak. Why hadn't she stayed out of the sun when she was younger? Now the experts were saying some sun was good for you. Coffee was good for you. You must eliminate trans fats. Lower your bad cholesterol. Raise your good cholesterol. Eat oatmeal. It was all so confusing. Though no longer prone to depression, there were days when Chick could almost see a black cloud above her head. Today had all the earmarks of one of those days.

Her stomach growled, reminding her of the dangers of a drop in blood sugar. I've got to shake off these demons, she thought, padding into the kitchen for a forbidden late night snack. Maybe a kiwi or two, whole grain crackers and hummus, something healthy.

"Oh, fuck it! I'm having a chocolate donut," said Chick out loud, pulling out the box of Yummy Delights hidden behind the canned goods. As she opened her mouth for the first delicious bite, of course the phone rang. She picked it up out of habit, forgetting to check caller ID. Happily, it was her old friend Pearl, her customarily booming voice blasted in Chick's ear.

"Chick, is that you? What's shakin'? You'd better be free this weekend cuz I'm invitin" you to come to Key West with me," yelled Pearl.

Chick's little heart leaped. A road trip to the Keys. She would go, absolutely she would. It had been years since she'd been there, one of her favorite places in all the world. Thoughts of her disappointing peace plans flew right out of her head.

"Oh, Pearl! How sweet of you . . . the Keys. Let me think for a minute . . . I did have plans on Saturday but I should be able to change them. Yes, I'd love to go!" In truth, she had nothing at all lined up, but she didn't want Pearl to think she was a complete dud with zero social life, especially since Pearl was a mover and a shaker, had buckets of money, a jet set lifestyle, and in Chick's opinion, far too many possessions. In fact, Pearl was the poster girl for conspicuous consumption. But Pearl was an old friend, had inherited her millions, spent lavishly on her pals, her whims, and herself, but pumped a lot of bucks into good causes, too. She lived in a big house on the Intercoastal

Waterway in St. Augustine when she wasn't off traveling the world. The rich were different, yes, but they were still people with the same hopes, dreams, aspirations and foibles as the rest of us. In short, they pulled their pants on one leg at a time. What this old adage proved or disproved was an unknown quantity, but it made the chicken feel better to think it. Among her own species, Chick had no wealthy friends or even acquaintances, but she supposed they were out there somewhere on the planet.

Pearl swiftly confirmed the arrangements. "Fantastic, Chick! I can't wait to see you. It's been way too long. I'll pick you up this Friday morning at 8:00 a.m. We'll make it to Key West for Sunset and a late dinner at Blue Heaven. Bring your dancin' shoes, girl! We are goin' out!" shouted Pearl.

And just like that, in the wink and the blink of an eye, Chick's world turned bright and beautiful. The moon came out. The stars twinkled. The music came on. She danced around and around the living room to her favorite Donna The Buffalo CD. Life was good!

5

On The Road Yet Again

As always, the night before anything exciting was happening the next day and she could use some good shut-eye, Chick barely slept a wink. Well before Pearl was due to arrive, she wheeled her suitcase out to the road to wait. She had packed and unpacked three times, tried on nearly everything she owned, hoping to come up with the beguiling and chic look she was going for, nearly forgetting the most important item, her new swimsuit.

Dang, was she still preening her feathers in search of Mr. Right? She quite enjoyed her single status, answering to no one, and free to do whatever she liked whenever she liked. But there were times, especially on chilly winter nights, when she longed for a companion to snuggle with. She did have many wonderful friends and here came one of them now to pick her up.

Pearl was right on time, looking splendid in her . . . her Hummer! Egads! Pearl was driving a brand new shiny black politically incorrect gas guzzling Hummer.

Oh, no. This can't be happening, thought Chick with

dismay. But it was happening. If she wanted to go to the Keys, she'd be riding in this environmental abomination that belonged in the Sahara Desert. Before she could even sputter a word, Pearl jumped out, grabbed Chick's bag, tossed it in the back, and in one swift movement shoved Chick's butt in the front seat, and buckled her in. They were off before Chick could even begin to protest, which, truth be told, she would not have, because she had her heart set on this trip. I can sacrifice my principles for this one teeny tiny weekend, can't I? she said to herself in a burst of pure selfishness. Yes, it takes a strong chicken to hold on to one's ethics in the face of desire and this time Chick succumbed to temptation.

In a short space of time, they were barreling south on I-75. It had been plenty of time, however, for Chick to remember that several years ago, she had vowed never to get in a car with Pearl as the driver, a sickening fact she had conveniently forgotten. Now, here she was trapped in a hated horrible Hummer with a lead-footed maniac!

The landscape was a blur that Chick couldn't see unless she were to stand up in the seat. "Oh, Pearl, I'm so sleepy. I think I'll just doze off a bit," said Chick, using a tactic that served her well in times of stress. She fell into a deep sleep, lulled by the sweet sounds of old Joni Mitchell tunes and Pearl's surprisingly good voice singing along. Hours later she was awakened by Pearl's finger jabbing her in the side.

"Wakey, wakey. Lunchtime, sweetie." Pearl spread out a sumptuous repast on a rest area picnic table under a shady tree. A yummy looking eggplant parmesan, kale salad, carob cake for dessert, all vegan, and a bottle of vintage red wine. It almost makes up for her driving, thought Chick as she wiped her beak on the pretty linen napkin.

"Two more hours to Key Largo," Pearl said as they cleaned up the remains of the meal and quite literally climbed into the huge vehicle, whose purchase Pearl began defending by some malarkey (in Chick's opinion) about carbon credit exchange, even though Chick hadn't brought up the subject. Perhaps Pearl was feeling a twinge of guilt. Chick was mortified just riding in the monster truck.

"That was a delicious lunch, Pearl, but it's putting me to sleep again. Please wake me when we're there," mumbled Chick, already nodding off as they pulled onto Alligator Alley. The next time Pearl poked her, they were turning into John Pennekamp State Park.

"Let's go for a swim, girlfriend!" said Pearl with her usual enthusiasm. They parked and found the bath house to change into their suits. Chick was reminded of a trip here twenty years ago with her friends, Bobbi and Teri. Darn, she also remembered looking pretty good in a bathing suit all those years ago, she thought as she caught a glimpse of herself in the mirror. She decided to put her shorts back on over her suit, even though she was wearing a slimming black Speedo. It wasn't enough to hide the bulging and sagging that were inevitable at her age, even with rigorous daily exercise which she didn't do. Pearl obviously felt the same way, as she emerged wrapped in a silky print sarong that covered her ample body completely. Yes, the days of bikinis for these two were over.

The protected swimming area was just as Chick remembered it, at least until she put her snorkel on. Sadly, there were definitely far, far less fish, she realized, dog paddling around in the salty water. Still, it was beautiful, the turquoise water, the azure blue skies, the clear clean air. As she floated on her back, toes pointed skyward, a feeling of peace washed over the little chicken.

"Oh, it's paradise, Pearl," she said as her friend swam up beside her.

"No, honey, this is gorgeous, but paradise is two hours south. Let's hit the road." The two toweled off, grabbed their clothes, and still clad in their damp suits, hi-tailed it back to the Hummer. Pearl fashioned a booster seat of sorts from the luggage so Chick could see over the dashboard.

"Sorry, sweetie. I forgot how little you were or I would have gotten you a car seat."

"Very funny, Pearl," answered Chick. It wasn't the first time someone had voiced this insulting suggestion. She had learned to ignore it.

The behemoth of a vehicle was nearly three feet above most of the other passenger cars on the road. Chick turned her head in shame when a couple wearing Greenpeace tee shirts glared up at them at a stoplight.

"It's not mine," she whispered to herself, but she felt culpable all the same. She wouldn't let it spoil her trip, she vowed and quite soon her concerns fell away, awed as she was by the sheer beauty of the vista before her, the smooth cerulean blue water, deepening to sapphire and ultramarine, meeting puffy white clouds at the horizon. The forty-two bridges stretched ahead, seeming to disappear and then a lovely little island popped into view, tiny cottages perched on the sand right next to . . . enormous new condos. Aaaagh! So ugly, a blight on the beach. The chicken had momentarily forgotten that she and Pearl would be spending the weekend in a new condo complex. No, I simply will not allow myself to dwell on anything negative for just this one weekend, she promised herself. Didn't she deserve a respite? A break from carrying the weight of the world on her small shoulders? A reprieve from wearing her heart on her sleeve? Yes, it was her turn to relax and unwind.

Chick spotted the sign first. 'Welcome To Key West', it said, and on the top stood a humongous statue of a chicken.

"I'm home, Pearl," Chick said to her friend, gazing at the sign, tears in her eyes. "This is my spiritual home. I love Key West."

Driving a tad slower out of necessity, Pearl pointed out various landmarks, the Lighthouse, the Hemingway home, The Nature Conservatory, the Southernmost Point, where they double-parked and jumped out for an obligatory photo op.

"What shall we do first?" squawked Chick, so excited she could barely contain herself. Pearl laughed.

"The first thing we do is get out of these wet clothes. We'll head over to the condo, freshen up and hit the streets."

Just when the little chicken thought things couldn't get any better, they did.

"Like it?" Pearl smiled as she opened the door. Chick's beak dropped in awe as they walked into the sunlit space. The condo was beyond gorgeous, right on the water, brand new, and designer decorated in an ultra-modern style.

"Here's your room, honey. You just fit right into this color scheme." The room was stark white with touches of red and yellow. On the balcony overlooking the beach, sat a glass table and chairs amidst a tangle of lush tropical plants.

"Could I just live here forever, Pearl?" Chick sighed as she flopped on the bed. "It's so beautiful."

"You can visit whenever you like, girlfriend. I'll give you your own key," laughed Pearl as she poured them both a glass of red wine. In another hour the pair were strolling down Duval Street with throngs of other tourists. And throngs of other chickens. For once, Chick wasn't the only chicken on the street. But she was the only one sporting a turquoise backpack and wearing a flowered sundress.

Yes, there were two thousand wild gypsy chickens strutting their stuff in Key West, Florida. It was wonderful. Chick was in heaven! She felt happy and safe. Gone was that uneasy nagging worry that kept her glancing over her shoulder even in Two-Lip. Here, as a chicken, she was revered and protected. All around her, in the streets, the parks, the old cemetery, were chickens. That they weren't dressed like her and didn't speak, at least in English, she barely noticed. They were her fellow beings, wild and free. How exhilarating and amazing life could be!

Giddy with happiness, Chick strolled proudly beside Pearl as they headed for Sunset at Mallory Square. Amidst crowds of tourists on the waterfront, they clapped in delight as the sun dipped below the water in a blaze of radiant orange and red. The only downer in Chick's opinion was the despicable man who coerced house cats to jump through hoops of fire and perform other humiliating tricks, undoubtedly trained by withholding food. Unlike dogs, felines did not enjoy performing for treats. A high-five and a few funny antics for a loving family was an exception. Chick had turned this fellow into the Humane Society in Atlanta a dozen years ago. Now here he was again, still plying his cruel trade. I'll have to deal with him when I get home, thought Chick. Another man with no compassion in his heart. Pearl seemed to think the show was cute, laughing along with the rest of the crowd.

Key West had a plethora of restaurants to choose from. The pair happily stumbled upon a vegetarian cafe called The Yard, where they stuffed themselves with the scrumptious fare. Old friends of Pearl's were arriving in town tomorrow and they would put off dining at Blue Heaven until the next evening. Off they went to watch the turtle races at Harry's where they had one too many cocktails, a beer at a tourist dive just for the cool music, enjoyed an ice cream from a street vendor, and near midnight, hailed a taxi back to the condo. Both of them quickly donned their jammies, neglected personal hygiene, and fell exhausted into a deep and peaceful slumber, lulled by the gentle waves breaking on the clean white sand.

Undaunted by the lack of sleep, the travelers sprang out of bed before 8:00 a.m., eager for the day ahead. They had twenty-four hours to cram in as much Key West flavor as they could. A glass bottom boat ride, a trolley tour, a visit to Nancy's secret garden, drinks at Hemingway's, naturally, a stop by the Chicken Store for souvenirs, and a slice of coconut cake at Bahama Village. Back at the condo, there was just time for a quick dip in the pool and a hot shower before the fun continued. Come evening, the two were decked out in their best duds and headed for Blue Heaven.

Sadly, this is the point where our story takes a ninety degree turn, where the idyllic little pastel colored bubble Chick had been floating in bursts, where illusions are cruelly shattered, and the grimy, seedy reality of life once again triumphs over a lovely dream.

The Blue Heaven! This charming iconic eatery came highly recommended and was jammed with tourists and locals alike. Pearl's friends from Vilano Beach, Charlene and Sunny, were waiting to greet them. The four sat chatting and drinking Bloody Mary's for close to an hour before being shown to a table. Chick was famished and ready for a great meal.

"Yum. Let's see . . . what looks good?" said Chick, opening her menu, almost drooling with anticipation. Carrot and curry soup, the Macro Bowl with quinoa and sweet potato, portobello mushrooms with black beans and rice? Oh. Oh, no! Her eyes froze and her beak dropped open. There, right in the middle of the menu under Entrees . . . CHICKEN . . . Jamaican jerk chicken.

"Oh!" gasped Chick. "Oh! Oh, no, no. But I thought . . . I thought." Her shoulders slumped and she dropped the menu on the table.

"What is it, Chick? What's wrong?" asked Pearl. Her companions looked at her with concern.

Chick wasn't born yesterday, as has been mentioned before. She was no spring chicken. She was well aware of the fact that ninety-five percent of people in the United States were meat eaters. Did she want to assimilate into mainstream society, to fit in despite her differences? The answer was yes. In Chick's opinion, there was a time and a place for announcing and discussing one's dietary preferences, one's culinary choices, one's hopes and dreams relating to the world's menu, but the dinner table was not the place.

"Oh, it's nothing of importance. I was mistaken, that's all," she said, masking her utter dismay with a smile. She wasn't about to put a damper on this little party. Inwardly devastated but relying on her innate social graces, she put on a happy face, swallowed her sorrow, and ordered the tofu. She prayed that no one at the table would order the chicken entree and thankfully, no one did.

The meal behind them, the foursome hit the streets. They were in and out of every bar on Duval Street. Chick danced with abandon long into the night. It wasn't until the drive back to the condo that she allowed herself to even think. In bed, she curled up in a ball and tried to sleep but she couldn't get that horrific menu out of her mind. People ate chickens in Key West, just not the Key West chickens. Chick had attempted throughout her life to educate folks, by example, by giving speeches, by joining animal rights organizations, seemingly to no avail. People wouldn't eat their pet dog or cat, but they gave no thought to eating a chicken, a far more intelligent species in her opinion. People wouldn't eat a canary or a parrot but they would eat a chicken. A chicken is also a bird, thought Chick bitterly. She knew full well that billions of these innocent beings were raised and slaughtered every year in the US alone. Living as a battery hen was every chicken's nightmare. Life as a free-range chicken in an enormously crowded facility wasn't far behind.

Chick, in her naivety, had briefly believed that in the tiny island paradise of Key West at the southern tip of her native country, chickens had found a true sanctuary. We all have our cross to bear. Her dream was short-lived but the hurt ran deep. I should have known better when I saw the giant yellow M, thought the chicken mournfully as she fell into a fitful sleep.

6

Home Again, Gone Again

Chick waved goodbye to Pearl as her friend peeled out of the driveway, tires screeching. The lucky bird had once again survived a trip with Pearl at the wheel. I love to travel but it's always good to come home, thought Chick as she opened her front door and headed for the kitchen. The first sight that confronted her was a sink full of dirty dishes.

"Yuck. I swear I did these before I left," she said out loud, searching for her favorite cup.

It feels like I've been gone for weeks, then in a day or so, it will seem like I never left, she mused, settling back with her mug of herbal tea in front of her computer. She received only three phone calls in her absence but she had seventy-nine new emails, not counting spam. Most were from political organizations or news sources like Common Dreams, True Majority, MoveOn, a few from friends, and several from Hillary and Chelsea. Back to reality, thought Chick. She couldn't face the possibility that Hillary might not win the nomination, but she fervently hoped there was still a chance. She was puzzled over the fact that so many women she knew were not backing the female candidate, yet she understood the total frustration with the Democratic Party, since primary votes in Florida or in Michigan were still not being counted. The situation was a mess. Each person's vote should count equally. A lover of polls and statistics, Chick followed a link from Huffington Post to the latest Presidential Poll.

"Aaagh . . . agh," Ms. Little groaned. Gallup polls showed McCain virtually neck and neck with Hillary and Barack Obama, nearly a dead heat. How could this be? Half the country was going to vote for another Republican? She thought of Henny. What was happening to her old friend?

Chick had pushed thoughts of Henny's strange behavior to the far recesses of her mind, along with her big peace plans. She felt a twinge of guilt at not keeping in touch, but it was after 10:00 p.m. and too late to call anyone. It was her general rule not to make phone calls after 9:00 p.m. or before 9:00 a.m., although she had friends with no such qualms. To prove that point, her phone rang. Caller ID showed her it was Goosey, and she picked up.

"What's new, Goosey?" Chick said as she answered.

"What's new with you, is the question. Tell me all about the Keys, you lucky girl. And nothing is new with me. I haven't sold a house in six weeks," lamented Goosey. Chick told her about the weekend in detail, leaving out the menu incident.

"I'd move to Key West in a heartbeat, if I could sell my house here," she told Goosey as she finished with her tale.

"Sure, honey, and I guarantee all you could buy would be a tin teepee smack up against some old geezer in a trailer park for the money you'd realize from your sweet little cottage in Two-Lip. And what about your friends? You may very well need them in your old age. Not that you're in your old age or anywhere close to it," added Goosey quickly, conscious of being quite a few years younger than

Chick. "Oh, I forgot, there is something new. You've never met the ditzy agent over at Redfern Realty, have you? Well, I know you don't like gossip, but . . . " Goosey launched into a long convoluted story about the sexual exploits of real estate professionals. Chick had to hold the phone away from her ear. I do like a bit of juicy gossip, she admitted to herself, but gee, let it be about someone I know.

"I'm beat, Goosey. I've got to get to bed," she finally told her friend, yawning loudly into the phone after several attempts at ending the long winded diatribe. "I'll see you on Wednesday at the Cup." Chick hung up. Life, she mused. The mundane daily soap opera struggle of most folks just to keep a roof over their heads and maintain a modicum of sanity in this crazy world. Thank the goddess, I don't live in China or Sudan or Burma. Was it called Burma any longer? No, she thought, it's called Myanmar now. She had always liked the magical name of Constantinople, but that city was now called Istanbul. It was hard to keep up.

She had one foot in her jammie bottoms when the phone rang yet again. Who on earth was calling at 11:15 p.m.? A number she didn't recognize appeared on the screen. Surely it wouldn't be a telemarketer at this hour? Intuition told her to pick up.

"Chick? Annie Miller from the coffee shop. Sorry to call so late, but I wanted to run this by you as soon as possible. You remember I mentioned a trip to Mexico, to San Miguel de Allende in early June? And you said how much you'd love to go? I've just learned there's a tiny extra bedroom at the place I've rented. Your share would be nominal. Of course you'd pay for your meals, but food is far less expensive in Mexico. Didn't you say you had a voucher on Delta? I've already checked and there are seats available on our flight. It would be my friend Mary, her daughter Julie, myself, and you, if you'd like to go. We'd all love for you to join us," said Annie.

How lucky could one chicken be! Chick barely gave it a thought before she said yes. Neither did she give any thought to the environmental impact of travel by plane.

"I haven't even unpacked from my last trip, but yes, I do want to go. Oh, Annie, thank you so much for inviting me," Chick replied warmly.

"Wonderful! It's nearly midnight and we're both tired. I'll fill you in on the details in the morning. Sleep well. Goodnight and may you have sweet dreams of old Mexico."

Is the universe smiling on me of late? pondered Chick as she lay in bed. I wonder why? Or is it just a random chance? A coincidence? Karma? It never rains but it pours, she thought, but that means misfortune, I think. Good things are happening to me. Anyhow, perhaps that old saying no longer held true. It hadn't rained in weeks except for a few pathetic sprinkles. The nearby lakes were drying up with alarming speed. She felt bad letting the water run long enough to get warm. Should she be practical and responsible and invest in a point-of-use water heater instead of taking this trip?

"No!" Chick exclaimed loudly. "I'm going to Mexico. Good fortune is smiling on me and I'm going to make the most of it."

7

Solo In Mexico

Chick and her three travel companions were perched on a rock wall under a shady jacaranda tree awaiting the start of the Dia de Los Locos parade. Translated to English it meant Day of the Crazies. They had arrived before 10:00 a.m. to secure this excellent viewing spot. Now it was high noon and our American girls were fidgety and restless.

"Wasn't it supposed to start at 11:00 a.m.?" Mary asked for the third time.

"Hey, mom. Chill," answered Julie. "We're on Mexican time."

Chick didn't mind the waiting. She'd already fallen in love with Mexico, with San Miguel and everything about it. Her head was chock full of plans and schemes to move here and become an expat. The town, the people, the architecture, it was all so alluring and captivating.

Last evening she sat sipping a bottle of Modelo on the roof of their casita and watched the fiery pink and orange sunset over dark blue mountains. The church steeples were awash in shades of ocher and gold, the houses all in a jumble of magenta and yellow, turquoise and mauve. Colors good enough to eat. Dogs barked, roosters crowed, strange blue-black birds screeched. A hummingbird hovered right in front of Chick's beak, momentarily mistaking it for a flower. She sat soaking in the luscious and foreign flavor of a culture far different from her own. To her, San Miguel appeared peaceful, relaxed, warm and loving. Yes, there were people begging in the streets, and she couldn't pass a person with an outstretched palm without dropping a few coins into that hand. Small children sold gum and trinkets in the jardin.

The city was a study in contrasts. It's like being in a movie, she thought for the hundredth time. She'd been here for a week and it felt like a lifetime. Her minimal Spanish came back to her when she needed it, which was frequently, since of course most folks spoke Spanish. She was spending a great deal of time on her own, as she simply could not keep up with the others, and was loath to take a taxi as a point of pride. The bird loved to walk, but let's face it, she was no match for a person with legs. By the time Chick had arrived at a restaurant, her friends had already eaten and she couldn't blame them. She had to scurry across the cobblestone streets as buses, trucks, cars, Jeeps and the popular ATVs made unexpected turns without benefit of traffic lights or stop signs, but it worked. She had yet to see an accident or road rage. Everyone was incredibly polite to each other and it warmed her heart. The Mexican people were so friendly, loving and happy. She knew that was a blanket statement, certainly not everyone was happy nor even well-fed, though it did seem that the locals in this town were more prosperous than in much of the country, for the most part due to the large influx of American dollars. Perusing the phone book, Mary had discovered there was no heading for mental health therapists. Surely Mexicans suffered from the same neurosis, fears, and phobias as her compatriots? Or did they? Life was different here. Even the birds were different.

At long last, with a bang and a clang and blaring horns, the Locos parade began. The biggest, most colorful, wild, and yes, the craziest parade the chicken had ever seen in her life. Scores of costumed characters jumped, clapped, sang and marched along to ear splitting music. People dressed as huge bugs, coal black cavemen, a bizarre bunch of diapered men and storks, every imaginable animal, including chickens, Bugs Bunny, Nixon, Cheney, and George Bush, all throwing candy, beads, and kisses. The town came alive with throngs of people, a sea of humanity, and an enormous variety of street food Chick and her fellow gringos were afraid to try. They could only drool at the huge bowls of sliced watermelon, papaya, and mango while tantalizing odors of frying tortillas assailed their nostrils. Chick, Mary, and Annie had already suffered through two episodes of the turistas, the cause of which could be anything, even water in one's mouth while showering.

Her diet was out the window. Chick relied on tacos and bean burritos as a staple. She could only hope that all the walking would compensate for the extra carbs and calories. Every idyllic day was crammed with new adventures. A highlight was a trip out to La Gruta Hot Springs. Cascading blue pools, high rock walls covered in bougainvillea, and a magical surprise, a long deep tunnel you swam through, ending in a high rocky dome of steaming water, a small beam of sunlight the only light source.

All too soon it was the last night for Mary and Julie. The four friends were gathered for a farewell dinner at Mama Luna, joined by a Canadian fellow named David they had met in the jardin. He does look a tad like David Niven, sporting a red nose. Probably a heavy drinker, Chick decided. She felt a twinge of jealousy as it was obvious that David was quite taken with Julie. He was old enough to be her grandfather, thought Chick indignantly, suddenly feeling every bit of her sixty-two years. When three of the party ordered steak, Chateaubriand nonetheless, she could barely hold her tongue. At least Annie was a vegetarian. They both ordered the portobello mushroom dish which was filling and delicious and hopefully not genetically modified. She soon let her irritation fade away as she enjoyed her wine and the soothing sounds of Lorna Davis, a jazz singer, long a fixture in San Miguel. Her lovely voice reminded Chick of Nina Simone.

Good friends, good food, good wine, a vacation in a foreign country. What more could one ask for? Yes, her life was indeed full. She was the luckiest of chickens.

Alas, plans are just that and the best laid plans can change in an instant. The next morning Annie was unexpectedly called back to the States for a family emergency. The others had departed and the rent was due for another week. Chick could either cut short her wonderful trip or gather her wits about her and find another less expensive casita. Luckily she had just learned to use her ATM card. The brave little chicken would be on her own in Mexico.

Chick was learning, one baby step at a time. She tossed her store-bought loaf of Bimbo Bread in the bin and bought a fresh baked whole grain offering at the Blue Door Bakery for fifty cents, and, at Ponderosa, an extra large bottle of SafeSure water purifier. She had again experienced an entire night of Montezuma's revenge, that unfortunate aspect of nearly any stay in Mexico. She had tried to be careful but her discomfort could possibly be traced to the raisins she sprinkled on her oatmeal. A new neighbor had told her to purify everything, even bananas. Everyone American had their own horror story involving their bowels, a subject rarely touched upon mornings at the Cup and Saucer back home. Yes, here in San Miguel one discussed with ease the state of one's digestive functions with people you met on the street. Amoebic dysentery with projectile vomiting was not a story to be told over coffee back in Two-Lip. Another mystery was the lack of refrigeration. Her fellow beings lay dismembered and quite warm in meat markets all over the city. What about salmonella? E-Coli? Carnivores deserved what they got, was the phrase that ran through her mind when gazing into the window of a butcher shop.

On a more cheerful note, last evening she'd been invited for cocktails by an American artist she and her pals had met on the mini-bus into town from the airport. Chick found she was still a bit weak from her tummy troubles when she could barely finish the horrendous climb up the hill behind Juarez Park to her destination. Thoroughly winded, she knocked at the brilliant azure blue double doors carved with a sun and moon, surrounded by angels. The door was answered by a maid, clad in the traditional black and white.

"Bienvenida, señora. Entrar, por favor." The lovely young woman greeted her with a dazzling smile and led her into the living room. Her host was Harriet Horner, a well known expat and benefactor of the Arts. The handsome woman sat on a plush sofa surrounded, to Chick's dismay, by her three dogs, who immediately came over to Chick and began sniffing her in all manner of private places. Their behavior was in stark contrast to the scrawny street dogs who barely glanced at her, thank goodness, intent on wherever it was they were going.

"Chewy, Millie, Lorenzo! Do leave our guest alone this minute," admonished Harriet. "So sorry, my dear. They're quite unaccustomed to a being of your size and stature, indeed of your species, except of course for their dinner!" chuckled Harriet. Chick decided then and there that she didn't like Harriet, but she was a guest in the insensitive woman's home and she would make the best of it, at least until she could make a graceful exit.

The sprawling adobe was worthy of a magazine, indeed

had been featured in *Architectural Digest* and was on San Miguel's House and Garden Tour. Massive rock walls, a tiled fireplace, glass bricks, skylights, enormous abstract paintings and sculpture, objets d' art filled the blue and purple house, replete with multi-terraced gardens overlooking the Parroquia and the setting sun. The small gathering was a cocktail party with several neighbors, a Canadian couple and their son, and a loud rather obnoxious heavyset man who obviously had too much to drink. Everyone was stuffing themselves with hors d'oeuvres, guzzling wine and beer, and downing shots of tequila. The only Mexican person present was the maid. Chick got a glimpse of local gringo culture, the culture of big money. This was one of the multi-million dollar homes that hung on the hillside of San Miguel overlooking the town and overlooking many Mexican citizens who could scarcely feed themselves, who rode into town by busload from the campos, hoping to find work, to sell their wares on the street, or to simply beg. Chick had seen a man with a bathroom scale charging a few pesos to weigh oneself, quite the entrepreneur. She struggled with what she perceived as a moral dilemma on a daily basis. On the one hand, the huge influx of wealthy Americans, Canadians, and Europeans living here brought jobs, commerce, ongoing financial support to the local economy, schools and programs for indigent Mexicans. On the other hand, even if the moneyed class were generous, how does one justify living in conspicuous luxury in the midst of dire poverty? How do the rich sleep at night? Yet, this was the way of the world, wasn't it?

Chick left the party as quickly as she could reasonably make an exit, trudging down the hill with these questions swirling around in her head. Her own rented casita looked very humble in contrast to her recent surroundings, yet she knew that to many working class folks, this small house would be considered lavish.

With the dawning of a new day, Chick faced her own problems. Much to her dismay, she still had to remain in close proximity to a bano. She dared venture out only after chewing four of the now indispensable pink tablets, wearing three pairs of underwear, and toting a change of clothes. One could never be too careful in these matters.

In a quandary about where she would spend the next week, she had rented new lodgings sight unseen. As the taxi driver deposited her and her luggage in front of the tall metal gates and sped away, Chick realized she could not reach the buzzer. She had no choice but to pound on the gates. After what seemed like an eternity, one of the other tenants let her inside. The charming courtyard was dense with tropical plants, Talavera tile work, and ivy covered coral walls. The elderly Mexican maid arrived, arms laden with fruit and flowers to welcome Chick. As the woman turned the key in the troublesome lock and opened the door, Chick saw with a sinking feeling just why the casita was so inexpensive. Unpretentious and quaint, the ad had said. Oh, dear, she had rented El Dumpo! Looking around, she took in the sorry sight, sagging furniture, a broken lamp, a bare light bulb on a frayed cord hung above a battered desk. Despite that, it was very clean, painted in pretty shades of blue, had a tiny bedroom, a dining room and a red and yellow kitchen. There is a certain charm, she reflected, trying to cheer herself up.

An hour later, she was having second thoughts as she waited for Martine, the handyman, to install new innards in the ancient commode, which had overflowed from the tank twice, flooding the living room. There was no phone. Luckily the woman who lived upstairs had a cell phone and was able to call la casera, the landlady. I wanted to be in El Centro, thought Chick, aware that she could have rented a lovely place a bit out of the center of town for the same money.

Can I really stay here for ten days? she asked herself nervously. Oh, dear.

Chick finally dragged her weary bones out of bed the next morning after a fitful and nearly sleepless night, ready to pay any amount of money to change her reservation and hop on a plane to the States, and she was homesick. The little bedroom had a damp musty odor, she couldn't open the window for lack of a screen to ward off the bloodthirsty mosquitoes, there was no water pressure, the shower and the bathroom sink merely a dribble. The propane stove was old and scary and the antiquated water heater for all four units continuously roared just outside her back door. She had spotted several crawling insects last night as she was about to retire and to top it off, as Chick pulled back the threadbare sheets on the lumpy mattress, a dead roach.

"Oh, help!" pleaded Chick. Someone was listening. Perhaps the goddess, perhaps the patron saint of gringo chickens alone in Mexico, maybe her personal guardian angel, but more likely it was the serendipitous nature of Chick's charmed life.

Unbeknownst to our precious little chicken, in a few short hours everything was about to change.

8

Sweet Old Pals

Chick sat on a lovely rooftop garden overlooking San Miguel, feet up, relaxed and content, sipping her morning coffee. Under an overhang, she watched the welcome rain drench the thirsty flowering and succulent plants on the jungle like patio. Life, once again, was good. Now her only problem was a lingering intestinal upset. Even that had nearly disappeared. Yes, thought Chick, lady luck has smiled on me once more, rescued me from the jaws of Hell, from a fate worse than death. That she could be overly dramatic in her thinking, even she herself would agree.

So, one might ask, how did Ms. Little come to be settled in this beautiful home when we last left her in the throes of a dilemma, unhappily ensconced in less than desirable lodgings?

A number of years ago, Chick had vacationed in San Francisco, staying for a week in a charming B&B run by an equally charming couple, Gavin and Emily. The pair had taken the chicken under their wing (no pun intended), showed her around the Bay Area, and had been not landlords but great pals during her stay with them. They had a large fuzzy dog named Bella, who was as gentle as a mother hen with Chick. Another member of the family was a West African gray parrot called Paco who had the run of the house and with whom Chick had many long conversations. The beautiful bird was quite content in the loving care of his human companions, having never known the jungle. He would sing Toscanini at the drop of a hat and loved to imitate Judy Garland. A genetic memory of soaring above verdant tree tops nagged at the far recesses of his brain only occasionally, a longing he could not quite put a claw on. Now the backyard aviary was his own private rainforest.

The friends had exchanged infrequent emails over the years, the last one from Emily detailing how disillusioned she and Gavin were with the political situation in the United States and that they were making a permanent move to Mexico, to the city of San Miguel de Allende. Chick had their contact information in town, but with the flurry of activities in the last week, had quite forgotten to get in touch.

The morning after her restless night in El Crummy Casita, the sweet faces of her old friends popped into her mind. Without a phone, she realized she couldn't even call to let them know she was here in Mexico. After a struggle pouring water from the huge jug in the kitchen, watching nervously as the propane stove sputtered and coughed, she was finally able to down two cups of lukewarm coffee, enough to fortify her for a walk across town to see if Emily and Gavin were indeed at home at that address.

Chick's rose colored glasses had slipped down her beak and her mood had slipped along with them. This morning the streets look dirtier, the stray dogs hungrier, the natives more destitute and the gringos richer, and speaking of slipping, Chick lost her footing on a wet stone walkway and landed smack on her derriere. Thoroughly embarrassed, she smiled bravely and profusely thanked the young Mexican man who kindly helped her to her feet. Style over sensibility, Chick admonished herself, knowing her poor choice of footwear was the cause of her fall. However did women walk in high heels? And why? She resolved to toss the offending fancy sandals and buy some sensible sneakers soon. She was far too old to be a slave to fashion.

With the aid of her newly purchased street map, she easily found Colegio, and Emily and Gavin's house number on Puente de Umaran. Just as Chick was about to ask a passerby for help to pull the out of reach bell ringer, the door opened. There was her dear friend Gavin, who instantly swept our feathered friend up in a big hug.

"Chick Little! Why, I can't believe it. Here you are in San Miguel. What a wonderful surprise! Come in, come in. I was going to the library but that can wait." Gavin led her into a cool high ceiling living room.

"It's lovely to see you again, Gavin. It's been eons. What a beautiful room!" said Chick looking around. "Is Em at home?" She suddenly realized how quiet the house seemed and how gaunt Gavin looked. And where were Bella and Paco?

"Yes, Chick. Emily is home, but sorry to say, she's quite ill. She got terribly sick on our trip back from California a few weeks ago and was in the hospital here for five days. A harsh case of food poisoning she ironically picked up in the States. It's rare to be hit so hard, but her immune system was compromised, unbeknownst to us. Thank goodness, she's on the mend now. No worries. Ruby's upstairs keeping her company. But Chick, I am sorry to have to tell you that we've lost our beloved parrot, Paco."

"Oh, no, Gavin. What happened?" she replied sadly.

"I don't know if you remember that we'd rescued him from a neglectful situation, from a hoarder who kept him confined in a small cage for years. The first veterinarian we took him to told us he was about thirty-five, but later on, the vet we came to use said he was probably much older. One morning he was simply gone, his old worn out body there on a pillow in his favorite window seat. We miss him terribly, but we think and hope his last years were comfortable," Gavin said softly.

"I'm so sorry for both of you. And yes, take it from me, I know Paco dearly loved you both and was very happy." Chick's voice was full of sympathy.

"I appreciate that so much, Chick. Now, tell me all about your trip. You look just as young as ever. Are you by yourself? How long have you been here? Where are you staying? You know you're welcome to bunk with us anytime," smiled Gavin.

"How about right now?" The question flew out of Chick's mouth without engaging her brain. She went on to relate her saga of the disastrous move to new quarters, trying to keep the story entertaining and lighthearted.

"Another San Miguel travel adventure for the Lonely Planet guide books," Chick finished up, laughing.

"Quite a story, Chick. Just let me tell Em you're here," said Gavin, getting up. "Can I get you some coffee?"

"No, thank you. I've had my daily quota, unfortunately. Listen, I'll just come back when Emily's up and around. I don't want to bother her."

"Hold on a second, I'll be right back, Chick. I do need to check on Em."

Chick sat back gazing around the striking room at the collection of pre-Columbian looking sculptures and contemporary paintings adorning the walls. Mexican handicrafts filled every nook and cranny. In a few minutes, Gavin returned.

"Go pack your bags, lady. Grab a taxi and come on over here. The guest room and downstairs bathroom are all yours. It'll be great to have you with us."

"Oh, no, Gavin. I couldn't possibly. I was only joking about staying with you," stammered Chick. "With Emily sick, I'd be in the way and imposing."

"No, you wouldn't, not at all. It will be good for Em and she welcomes you here. And we certainly don't want you to leave our beloved city of San Miguel with bad feelings. Now, here's your key to the front door," said Gavin firmly. "Just let yourself in."

With a light step and a joyful heart, Chick trotted across town, threw her things in her suitcase willy-nilly and left the dreaded dump without a backward glance. She took the fresh flowers.

9

Cool, Curious, and Courageous

The roof garden of her friend's beautiful home had quickly become Chick's favorite place. Nearly finished with her coffee, she sat looking through Hola!, the weekly English language newspaper, hoping to find an entertaining activity for the day. Standing up to stretch her wings, she couldn't help but notice a naked man on the adjacent roof hanging out his laundry. Mexico! Technically, he is in the privacy of his own home, thought Chick to herself. Laws in Mexico regarding nudity were constantly changing. In the years to come, Mexico City would hold a Naked Day Parade through town. The city of Guadalajara would make sex in public legal, as long as no one filed a complaint. Mexico was a deeply religious country but far more accepting of the human body than the puritanical USA. I'm not one to complain, thought Chick as she admired the man's buff physique. Nice butt. Still . . . what an exhibitionist. Men!

Now, what would she do today? She considered her options. A walk through the market, a nice lunch, then the Biblioteca at 2:00 p.m. for a movie? That was the library, though it was nothing like a library in the States. You could bring your dog, relax in the open courtyard, shop in the tiny gift store, get a bite to eat in the restaurant, or take in a movie. Today's offering was a documentary and a talk by a local resident, Ruthanne Ross, examining why she and so many Americans lost their heart to San Miguel. Chick could relate. Arriving late as usual, she found a seat in the crowded room near the back, spending a few pleasant hours. But afterward she realized the presentation was most certainly geared toward people with far more excess funds than she herself possessed. She did buy the DVD to share with her buds back home. We'll have a party at Junie Moon's and show it on her sixty-inch wide TV, thought Chick with a twinge of homesickness.

Making her way back to the house, she stopped at Ponderosa, a fifteen by forty foot grocery store that to her amazement stocked everything one needed except fresh produce, found in abundance in the mercado. All could be had at a fraction of US costs, but still would be too expensive for a Mexican family of little means. An enormous new food market, GiganteMart, sat on the edge of town and, to Chick's horror, another huge American chain store was going up by the bus station. What would happen to the myriad family run tiny tiendas, indeed all the small businesses, when this greedy behemoth opened its doors? Financial devastation for the small business person, the same fate anywhere these monstrous corporations invaded. Chick's busy little head was already designing boycott bumper stickers and organizing protests.

It was after 8:00 p.m. when she returned to her friend's home, but Emily had just gotten out of bed. Ordinarily Em was a person with boundless energy and it was shocking to see her so weak. Gavin helped her up to the roof terrace and the three sat watching the orange sun set over spiraling gold domed steeples. There was even a glimpse of the famed Parroquia lit up like a Christmas tree. The old dog, Ruby, ambled up to join them. At fourteen, she was nearing the end of her life. Yet another sad loss looming ahead for the couple.

Gavin cooked dinner again as he did nearly every night. Chick didn't want to be a burden but she couldn't turn down the offer of a tasty and nutritious meal. She stood on a chair at midnight quietly washing the dishes, pots and pans. Not being much of a cook herself, cleaning up was the least she could do to repay her friend's hospitality.

The days passed in a blur of activity, endless shopping for trinkets, a tour of a glass factory, lunches and chats with people she met around town, and a marvelous dance recital at the Maria Martinez Theater. Dancers from four to sixty-four! Granted, the songs would have had more meaning if Chick had a better grasp of Spanish. But it was great rowdy fun with the audience frequently shouting loud salutations and encouragement. Music truly is a universal language, she knew without a doubt. Here in Mexico, scratchy loudspeakers blared tunes and fireworks boomed and sparkled, in celebration of anything and everything, even the dawn of a new day.

The next evening, Chick ventured out on her own, meeting new friends at Harry's Bar for a round of drinks. There were two men in the group of a dozen women. Prospects for a romantic liaison in this town were dim. Women outnumbered men in San Miguel, especially among the expats. No matter, I could live here, she thought to herself dreamily, splurging on a taxi ride home. The fare was only three dollars and it had begun to drizzle. She was sharing the ride with an acquaintance from the bar who lived in the same direction. Rather abruptly, Chick was asked to get out before her destination, so the driver could avoid a long one way detour. Taken by surprise, she only realized later that she should have said no.

"Muy cerca! Muy cerca," said the driver, pointing a finger out the window as Chick climbed out of the taxi.

"I may as well have walked," she muttered as she picked her way along the bumpy cobblestones on the suddenly unfamiliar street. Where am I? thought Chick, looking around with a twinge of alarm. This corner should be Aparicio but it wasn't. She walked a block further and the sign read Animus, a street she didn't know at all. Remembering she had passed a still open tienda when exiting the taxi, she began to retrace her steps. But after two blocks when she arrived where she was sure the welcoming light had been, all was shut tight, the huge wooden doors lining the dark street closed and foreboding.

"Oh, why didn't I bring my map? Why didn't I buy a cell phone that worked in Mexico?" Miserable, she stumbled along, now unsure of which direction she should take at all. Totally confused, she turned at yet another unknown corner, and then another. Oh, dear, I'm doing just what all the guidebooks say not to do. I'm a chicken walking alone at night on a dark street. Chick bit her bottom beak. I will not cry, she told herself. This is silly. She struck out blindly in the pitch black, looking down to avoid falling into a gringo hole, when a shadowy shape above her blocked out what little light there was. Chick froze, her heart in her throat, ice in her veins and looked up.

"Why, it's the little chicken!" said a melodious voice high above her. "How nice to see you again."

Apprehensive and jittery on the dim streets, Chick squinted up into the darkness. The voice sounded familiar, but was it anyone she knew?

"It's Lorna Davis. I'm the singer from Mama Luna," said the woman kindly. "Whatever are you doing out here so late?"

"Oh, Lorna!" Chick breathed a sigh of relief. "I'm so happy to see you. I'm . . . I . . . I think I'm lost."

"Yes, it's very easy to get confused in this maze of streets. The same thing happened to me when I first arrived. Now, what's your address?"

Chick's mind was blank but she finally managed to dredge up the correct street and house number.

"Why, we're practically neighbors," said Lorna. "Come on, I'll walk you home."

Half an hour later, Chick was safe and sound, in her nightie, beak brushed and climbing into her cozy bed. Another crisis averted, she thought, as she dozed off into dreamland. I truly do lead a charmed life for an old bird.

The next morning Emily felt well enough for an outing. The friends piled into the Prius to visit Em's new horse, Little Blue. Chick was less than thrilled, envisioning herself the object of an ill placed kick, but Em assured her that the horse was polite and well-mannered. Blue was a sweetheart, but simply enormous next to the chicken. She declined the offer of a ride without divulging her secret. She had never been on a horse and never intended to be, unless one counted merry-go-rounds.

Much too soon, only three days of her trip remained and she meant to make the most of it. I want to do something meaningful, she thought, as she flipped through Hola!

An unusual notice caught her eye. Mattress Making at St Paul's Church 10:00 a.m. Volunteers needed and welcome. If Chick got moving, she could just make it on time, even walking. This time she would bring her map.

Six women, one man and a goose sat around a large table as Toni, the head of the project, explained what was involved. Each of them would twist up clean plastic shopping bags, trapping a bit of air in a loose knot. The bags would then be stuffed into a sturdy fabric cover sewn by other volunteers. One thousand of the plastic knots made a child size mattress. It was a clever way of recycling the plethora of single-use plastics produced. These comfy beds were then distributed to needy families out in the campos and to remote orphanages high in the mountains.

"What a worthwhile project," Chick said to the group seated at the long table. "I'm happy to help."

To Chick's joy and delight, one of the other helpers was a bilingual goose named Gansa, who had recently moved to San Miguel. Oh, how Chick missed Goosey Loosey and Henny, too. She and Gansa hit it off right away and when the mattress making had finished, headed over to El Mochahetas for a savory meal of enchiladas drenched in mole sauce and ensalada. What good fortune for each of them to have found a comrade, another farm animal that had assimilated into society. Their kind were few and far between, a mystery that had yet to be solved by science. The pair hoped this was to be the start of a lifelong friendship.

The next day she and Gansa booked a day trip to the city of Guanajuato, the nearby town some thought the most beautiful in Mexico, the houses painted in every color of the rainbow. The enchanting city was the birthplace of Diego Rivera. The two paid a visit to his childhood home, now a museum. Gansa and Chick giggled at the sight of such a tiny crib for a baby who turned out to be a giant of a man. Frida and Diego! Just as in the states, Frida's image was everywhere, her work reproduced on tiles, tee shirts, napkins, and posters. Her artwork had become a money generating commodity. Chick wondered what the artist would think, her self portrait adorning an oven mitt or a toilet paper roll.

Returning to San Miguel as the sun was setting, the two agreed this town, a haven for artists and writers, was still their favorite. The long day at an end, Chick squeezed back tears as they said their goodbyes.

"Come to Two-Lip, Gansa! I'd love for you to meet my friends. You'd fit right in. Send me an email soon," waved Chick.

Our little chicken's last day in Mexico was full. She finally connected with a friend of Turkey's from Palm Beach who treated her to yet another delicious lunch, homemade chili rellenos at her condo. The complex was all too modern, bland, and white for Mexico, in Chick's humble opinion.

"Stay with me anytime, Chick. This would be your room," said Sheila, opening the door to a pretty but plain room overlooking the manicured lawns. One had to remember that this was Mexico. The setting could be Florida or California.

"How kind of you," answered Chick. She appreciated the invitation but knew she would never accept. Privately she viewed the sprawling newly built condo complexes as part of the unfortunate gentrification of San Miguel. While not the most expensive destination in Mexico, San Miguel was far from the least. The town was growing. Every time new construction of the sterile variety went up, the town lost a bit of its character.

Chick packed her bags late that evening after a quiet dinner with her wonderfully helpful friends, who by their generosity had saved her from the undesirable lodgings. She left most of her clothes for the maid, Lupita, to give to her children and filled her suitcase with metal nichos, coconut dolls, and a kilo of milagros. At 1:00 a.m., Chick sunk her head deep into the memory foam pillow and settled in for a few hours of sleep before her airport pickup at 5:00 a.m. Images of San Miguel and the faces of her friends, old and new, flitted before her eyes as she fell into a peaceful slumber. Now it's Mexico I'll be missing was her last thought as she drifted off. She didn't hear the mosquito buzzing around her ear, nor did she hear the gentle rain that fell for hours, polishing the stone streets to a shiny sheen.

Nor did she hear her alarm. She awoke with a start, fifteen minutes to spare, had to hurriedly grab her things and scramble bleary-eyed and half asleep to the door with her suitcase and no coffee. Chick left the house key on the hall table, saying a silent farewell to Emily, Gavin and Ruby. She quietly shut the front door behind her and stood waiting outside for her ride, for the dawn of a new day, and the next chapter in her life.

10

The Big Surprise

Near midnight of the long day, Chick relaxed in her favorite chair, sipping a glass of sweet sangria. Bone tired and woozy from her three different flights home, she was, as usual, vowing to never do it again. I'll just be content at home working in the garden and watching the birds, she thought, forgetting that she always felt this way after returning from a trip.

"Gee, I hope I didn't forget to pay my house insurance," she said with a groan, spying the huge stack of mail her neighbor, Junie, had piled on the hall table. Along with the mail was a welcome home gift of homemade peanut butter fudge, her favorite.

"How sweet of her," said Chick out loud, as the delicious treat melted in her mouth. She flipped through the mail, hoping not to see anything marked Final Notice. There was a letter from Bernadette in New York, a postcard from her old boyfriend Michael, the usual assortment of junk mail, pleas from charities Chick donated to when she had any spare dollars, and . . . what was this? A square pink envelope with an Oberlin, Ohio return address, and above it, P. Little.

Why, that's my last name, thought Chick, confused. She stared at the unfamiliar address, finally turning it over and, using her fancy silver letter opener, slit it open.

'Dear Chick,' the letter began. 'I know this will come as a shock to you after so many years. My name is Precious Little and I am your sister. I've spent considerable time tracking you down since I first learned of your existence. I believe, in fact, I am quite certain that you are the right Chick Little. I was unable to obtain a phone number for you nor an email, hence this letter. I am very anxious to speak with you, in part because I will be in Gainesville on the twenty-fourth of this month and I see that you live nearby. I do hope you are in receipt of this letter and will be able to meet with me that morning before my conference begins, as my schedule after that will be crowded. I suggest you call my hotel, the Marriott, and leave a message, at your earliest convenience. I am so looking forward to meeting you. Your loving sister, Precious.'

"Oh, my God!" cried Chick. She swallowed the rest of her wine in a huge gulp, her feelings a mixture of disbelief, pleasure and dread with a tad of suspicion thrown in. How could this be? I'm sixty-two years old. I have a sister I've never met and she found me. How? Maybe it's a scam targeting senior citizens, thought Chick suddenly. Older chickens could never be too careful. Well, I'll just call her tomorrow and . . . wait a minute. Getting here on the twenty-fourth? What's the date again? Of course, she had just returned from Mexico today, the twenty-third. And that meant her sister, her sister would be arriving tomorrow!

"Oh, my God!" Chick said yet again, falling back on the much overused phrase of the day. This was all entirely too much. "Should I call her now? No, no, I don't want to wake her up." Even though it was now, after midnight, she had to tell someone. The chicken picked up the phone and punched Goosey on speed dial.

"Hellooo," answered Goosey in her best professional realtor voice, ever on the lookout for new clients no matter the hour.

"Hey, it's me! I'm back from my trip and I have amazing news," screeched Chick into her phone.

"Oh, no, honey, please don't tell me you're moving to Mexico. I just knew it. Oh, I don't want you to leave," wailed Goosey

"No, no, Goosey. It's not that at all. It's . . . it's . . . I have a sister," Chick exclaimed. "And she'll be here tomorrow!"

11

The Wonderful Reunion

Exhausted as she was, Chick slept soundly, the morning sun shining through her window teasing her awake. She lay in her cozy bed, drifting in and out of dreams, musical wind chimes playing a lovely tune, drums keeping time to the beat. Suddenly, Chick sat bolt upright, fully awake. Once again, she'd slept through her alarm.

It's the doorbell, she realized, and someone knocking, not drumming. With apprehension and a sinking certainty, she knew who it must be. Clad in her comfy old threadbare, coffee stained nightie, she stumbled to the door.

Her sister! Yes, there on the doorstep stood a beautiful coal black chicken, just a hint of white at the tips of her feathers, looking smart and stylish in a tailored pants suit and Ferragamo pumps.

"Oh, dear, I thought you'd be white," blurted Chick.

"And I thought you'd be black," answered the chicken. "When I didn't hear from you, I decided to take a chance and Uber out here." They both began laughing as they fell into each other's wings. All doubts on Chick's part flew out the window, so immediate was the unmistakable connection. After a long and tearful hug, she finally disengaged herself, apologizing for her morning breath and unsightly bedhead.

"I'll just put on some coffee," said Chick, backing up. "I know it seems like I'm awake, but I'm merely sleepwalking without my java."

"Do you have a spot of tea, Chick? If it's no trouble, I'd much prefer it." Chick suddenly realized her sister didn't sound like an American.

"But . . . you speak with a British accent. I don't understand," said Chick, puzzled. The sisters headed for the kitchen, and as Chick prepared the coffee (and tea!) Precious began to explain.

"When I was only a few days old, barely hatched, I was adopted here in America. My adoptive father was employed by a European oil company and when I was still a baby, he was transferred to the UK. I grew up in Wales, so yes, I do have an accent," said Precious in her sweet lilting manner. "My husband and I spend half the year in Great Britain and the other half here in the States. I teach physics at Oberlin College in Ohio and also lecture at Oxford in England where I did my post graduate work. I met my husband Alfred in Italy when we were working on our doctorates."

Oh, dear, thought Chick to herself. I was lucky to get my GED.

"I don't have much formal education," she said in a small voice.

Precious smiled kindly. "I'm over-educated, believe me. It hasn't resulted in riches. I'm fortunate that Alfred does well as a music producer. And I can tell by looking around your charming home that you love books and music and art. We have a lot in common, dear sister," said Precious, walking into the living room. She picked up a framed picture. "And who are these darling three?"

"That's my girl, Dahlia, and her two boys when they were a bit younger," Chick said proudly. "They live down south in Sarasota. I can't wait to tell my daughter about you!" exclaimed Chick.

Precious looked at her sister with tears in her eyes. "I have a girl, too. and she has two sons, also." She got her purse and pulled out a picture remarkably similar to Chick's own.

"All the years we've missed," said Chick as she looked through the batch of pictures Precious had spread out on the kitchen table. Herself as a baby chick, her teen years, her wedding, the birth of her children. Chick choked back a sob.

"I know it's so very sad," answered her sister. "But let's not dwell on what might have been. We've found each other now and hopefully we'll have many years of making new memories."

Chick gazed at Precious, her heart filling up with love and gratitude. "I finally found my long lost family."

"And I feel the same way," said her sister. "I'm thrilled and beyond grateful to have you back in my life."

The sisters talked the day away, sharing stories of their respective lives, exchanging and taking many silly and serious photographs, and reminiscing. Neither bird could remember their mother. They had only been newly hatched chicklets when they were all separated. Although she had searched, Chick was the only sibling Precious had been able to locate. They briefly touched on Chick's upbringing.

"That's a long story for another day, Precious," she said with a frown.

"I respect that, Chick. Whenever you're ready, I under-stand." Chick's heart swelled. Her sweet sister was so full of empathy, compassion, and love.

"But, Chick," Precious continued. "I do want to know more about your life. You said you're divorced. How long were you married? And is he Dahlia's father?"

"My ex-husband's name is Bud," said Chick with a fond smile. "No, he's not Dahlia's dad. He's a kind man, truly a wonderful man. We were together for twenty years. We just grew apart and to be truthful, both of us had an affair. We forgave each other and tried to reconcile, but there was just too much water under the bridge. Cloudy and murky water," said Chick ruefully. "But we're good friends. I do miss him. He's returned to the Pacific Northwest and hasn't been back to Florida in years. You would have liked him, Precious. I guess monogamy isn't for me." Chick finished up her tail with a grimace.

"My goodness, Chick. I'd say twenty years is a pretty good run. Maintaining a long-term relationship is difficult to say the least. Sometimes it's best to let go and move on. It's wonderful and speaks to both of your characters that you've been able to maintain a friendship. So many marriages end in acrimony. Don't think for a moment that Alfred and I haven't had our ups and downs."

Once again, Chick was thankful for her newly found sister's compassion and lack of judgment. Her heart brimming with joy, Chick jumped up.

"Let's go dancing tonight! We can go to the Kickin' Devil. I know the band, Horseplay. They're awesome. You'll love them!" Chick enthused, forgetting that Precious had mentioned a preference for classical music and opera.

"My friend, Goosey, loves to dance. She'll want to go, I'm positive. She can drive us and then drop you off at your hotel." Chick reached for the phone. "It will be so much fun!"

And that's exactly what they did. The geriatric chickens and the goose were a huge hit with the college kids, their dance card always full. All three rocked out and danced with wild abandon, ignoring their sore feet. Precious left her conservative manner at the edge of the dance floor. She knew how to let loose and have fun. Chick's ego soared when a handsome young man told her he thought she was the prettiest girl in the room. He meant chicken, she was sure.

As she and Goosey drove Precious back to the Marriott, Chick had a brilliant idea. "Could you stay a few more days after your seminar, Precious? I really want to take you kayaking on the Ichetucknee. It's my favorite river in all the world and I'd love to share it with you. We can go on Monday. Please say yes!"

"Oh, Chick. I'd love to. I will. I'll arrange it," Precious responded impulsively. "Today has been marvelous. More than I ever hoped for. And Chick, please start planning for a trip across the pond. You simply must come to Wales," she said, getting out of the car. "I love you, dear sister. See you on the Monday."

12

River Run

Promptly at 7:00 a.m. on Monday morning, Katie pulled her truck into the driveway, honking the horn. Chick was fully awake, having downed her coffee, and Precious, her tea. Goosey had volunteered to drive to Gainesville yet again and bring Precious back to Two-Lip on Sunday night. The two sisters were ready to go, clad in Columbia sportsgear, courtesy of the church thrift shop, wide-brimmed hats, refillable water bottles, lunch and whistle in wing, and a sense of humor, all essentials for a day on a Florida waterway.

As always, it would be a surprise to see who showed up at Cavallini's gas station, the kayak rendezvous. Chick was hoping for a good turnout so Precious would feel safe and secure for her maiden kayak voyage. Her sister had voiced fears of alligators and snakes, and though she was a good swimmer, nervous about overturning the kayak.

"No one's ever seen an alligator on the Itch, " Chick said reassuringly, although she wasn't really sure of the truth of that statement. She did know that her friend Clark, a veteran kayaker, had never seen one in a lifetime on this particular river.

"Just look, you have all of us to protect you," she said waving her wing at the large group who stood waiting to leave. There was Brad, Rob, Bob, Louis with his canoe, Crazy Lizzie, Stormy, Ducky, Rocky, Suzy, and Clark, co-owner of the iconic store. Clark immediately upon their arrival had literally swept Precious off her feet with his charm, good looks, and strong arms. He and his brother, Chip, were fixtures in Two-Lip. The station was a hangout for the weird and wonderful of the area ever since their father had opened the store in 1935. A full service gas station, one of the last to survive, a bait shop and a bar rolled into one. You could drink a beer outside, and on weekends, dance to local musicians set up on the patio. It was old Florida with all the charm of days gone by

It's too bad Clark is married, thought Chick for the umpteenth time, as she sat next to him in his Range Rover, Precious beside her. Clark was the head of the group, and the lead vehicle in a long line of trucks and SUVs, snaking through the back roads and small towns of rural Florida toward the headsprings outside of Fort White. In summer, the river was jammed with tubers, but today, in all likelihood, they would have the pristine river all to themselves. It was a perfect day, sunny with billowy white clouds, little wind, no rain in sight, and no rain predicted.

The struggle to unload and launch the boats was always a challenge, always some mishap, a cell phone in the water, an item forgotten, a slippery misstep, and today was no exception. Chick and Precious planned to ride in Katie's kayak and were nearly ready to launch. Then, as Rocky was getting into his new kayak and Rob was attempting to hold it steady, Rocky, his phone, his camera, and his lunch slipped right in between the dock and the boat.

"Chilly! But off to a pretty good start." Rocky laughed

it off, sputtering as he retrieved his belongings. "I hear you can dry out these phones in a bag of rice." Always positive and not one to complain, Rocky was fun to be around. Now, if that had been Ducky that took an unplanned dunking . . . Chick shuddered, contemplating the probability of an unpleasant scene.

"You girls should come with me in my canoe if you want to avoid getting wet," warned Louis with a grin, directing the remark to Precious. He maneuvered his boat up close to the dock, flashing his most winning smile.

"Then it wouldn't be a kayak trip, Louis. I want my sister to experience a kayak," explained Chick. He's such a philanderer, she thought, always after the latest woman on the scene, spiriting her off away from the others. Louie the Lech, she said to herself uncharitably. As if to prove it true, Louis said with a wink, "I'll just take Precious if you don't want to come, Chick." And just like that, her sister, apparently smitten, hopped into the big canoe without a backward glance, saying, "Fine with me. It looks way more stable."

Louis actually stuck his tongue out at Chick as he paddled off in his usual style, intent on overtaking the others. She was flabbergasted. Everything had changed so quickly. Then Katie had to run back to her truck for a shirt. Now they were the last to leave the dock.

"Let's get going!" urged Chick. "Oh, dear. We're so far behind them," she said anxiously. "Could you paddle faster, Katie?" She straddled the bow of the kayak, perched between the row of plastic ducks adorning the front of Katie's boat. Searching in vain for a glimpse of the bright yellow canoe, she was barely able to enjoy the serene beauty of the crystal clear water, the bubbling turquoise springs, eel grasses waving on the white sandy bottom, silvery schools of mullet flashing brightly as they jumped for reasons of their own. Turtles sunned themselves on fallen logs, a dozen in a row, so used to the silent boats, they stayed put unless you ventured into their comfort zone. The river opened up and wild rice grasses swayed gently as flocks of coots called to each other, seemingly in unison. Alas, all this beauty went unseen and unappreciated by our dear little chicken, caught up as she was in a state of anxiety.

"Chick! Stop fretting. Chill," Katie finally admonished her. "Louis is quite capable. Stop rocking the boat!" Chick was twisting and turning, trying to see ahead. Rocky paddled up beside them and offered a toke on his sweet home grown bud.

"Here, little chickadee. This will help," he said, tuning in on Chick's worried look. At first she shook her head no, but in a flash of insight, accepted the offer, taking too big a hit, which caused her a fit of coughing. The effect on her thinking was nearly immediate. *I'm being silly and overprotective. Precious is a grown chicken. But I do feel responsible. I can't believe she'd just take off like that,* fumed Chick. *I really don't know her at all. Do I know myself? Who am I? What is my true nature? Do I have a fear of flying? I never fly anymore. I'm in a rut. What will I do with the rest of my life?* As always, smoking weed brought introspection and an initial bit of paranoia.

Shortly, in a pleasantly altered state of mind, she sat back, relaxed, and watched the river flow, her thoughts now a peaceful daydream. *Mother Nature is a miracle, a marvel, beautiful beyond words. The earth is a paradise and I'm so content and grateful to . . .* "Awkkk!!"

Chick nearly slipped off the bow of the boat, as Louis jumped out from behind a clump of tall grass in front of the kayak, wildly flapping his arms.

"Where have you been, slowpokes?" he bellowed, laughing. Precious and the others were splashing about in the cool water.

"Come for a swim, Chick! Put on the mask. You can

see the springs bubbling up, and there's even a cave down there," called her sister excitedly. "It's utterly fantastic. I saw an alligator gar. What a funny looking fish. I've never snorkeled before and I love it. And I love your wonderful friends, too," she said, glancing pointedly at Louis. Chick saw a look past between them, intimate and sensual. Or was it her imagination? That was fast, thought Chick. And weren't they flirting at the station this morning, too? Louis was single, divorced and a well-known playboy about town. In another burst of insight, Chick realized she was jealous, an ugly emotion she had thought behind her. Yes, to be honest with herself, she'd always enjoyed Louis's innuendos and outright invitations to sleep with him. He had a neat compact body, very short and muscular, closer in size to her own diminutive stature than most men. She had turned him down repeatedly, not wanting to be another notch on his belt, another feather in his cap. He liked older women, she had heard. He liked all women. He liked chickens. He liked Precious.

Chick looked jealousy right in the eye and resolved to let it all go. Tune into her higher self. Tap into her inner wisdom. It's my wounded ego, she thought accurately. I can do better. For the remainder of the day on the river, she savored every moment, basking in the joy of nature's bounty, of her dear friends, her new family and her good fortune.

The sisters rode back to Gainesville in Katie's truck. The drive was fun yet bittersweet. The three sang along to an old Carole King CD they all knew by heart. None of the trio were singers. In fact, they were tied for the worst voice. No one in the truck would be auditioning for American Idol in this lifetime.

Forty-five minutes later they pulled up in front of the Marriott. It had been a day the sisters would always remember. A short tearful farewell and Precious was gone, the doors of the hotel sliding closed behind her. They would see each other again soon, hopefully in Wales in the springtime. We've been blessed by the universe, the sisters agreed. Who or how or what did the blessing is the great mystery of life. Was it destiny? Was it pure coincidence? A twist of fate? Or part of a grand master plan?

While their reunion was a story worthy of an appearance on Oprah, they were both mortified at the idea. It was one thing to share their joy openly with loved ones, quite another to reenact an emotional life-changing event for lip smacking public consumption. Their story would remain private.

Much later that night, as Chick collapsed exhausted into her bed, she said out loud and not for the first time and not for the last time, "I am one lucky chicken."

13

Family Girl

Enjoying a few more luxurious minutes in her warm bed, Chick lay there wiggling her toes, feeling lazy. She had yet to unpack from her Mexico trip. It was still with a sense of the incredible when she replayed the joyful reunion with her sister. Their reuniting was all so amazing and, as they say in Britain, brilliant.

The ringing phone jolted her out of her reverie. I wish I could remember to turn it off at night, she said to herself, but in truth she was reluctant to do so. What if Dahlia or the boys needed her? What if one of her friends had an emergency? What if a tornado was bearing down on the town of Two-Lip? Chick saw herself as a realist but her pals called her a worrier, always fretting over what if.

"Hola?" said Chick into her phone, a hello in Spanish slipping out unbidden.

"Mom, what? It's me." The caller was Dahlia, her precious progeny, as Chick liked to think of her. And now she had another precious thing in her life.

"I only have a minute to talk, Mom. James is coming

down from school this weekend and he could swing by and pick you up, give you a ride back on Sunday. Is your sister still there? She's my aunt, you know. I want to meet her," said Dahlia briskly.

"Oh, honey, she had to leave. I'm sure you'll meet her soon. She doesn't look much like me but I think she looks like you. Or you look like her. Or, oh, I don't know, I haven't had my coffee yet. We took a million pictures." Chick felt a stab of conscience. Should she have taken her sister down to Sarasota instead of on the kayak trip? No, of course there wasn't time. Chick had called and left a garbled message and Dahlia hadn't returned her call. Why did she feel guilty?

"I don't quite see how I'm going to meet her soon if she lives in Great Britain. But, Mom, I'm busy. You can tell me all about it when you get here. Got to go. Is 4:00 p.m. on Friday good for you?"

"Yes, wonderful. I'd love to come down for a visit, sweetie," answered Chick. She was thrilled at the opportunity to spend an afternoon with her oldest grandson. She didn't see much of him now that he was away at college. Chick thought wistfully of her countless nights of babysitting when the boys were little. Dahlia was a hard worker but she did like to party in those days, sometimes returning in the early morning hours. Chick was glad the middle of the night diaper changes and 5:00 a.m. bottles were behind her. James and his younger brother, Zach, were the cutest babies, now handsome young men. Grown up, the boys barely remembered to call her. In all honesty, a call from either boy was rare. They have their own lives, thought Chick, using a well-worn phrase. Still, it made her feel a bit sad. This weekend would be a treat. Chick pushed thoughts of Dahlia's big black dog, Tek, to the back of her mind where he lurked expectantly, as if waiting for a chance to pounce.

The doorbell rang promptly Friday at 4:00 p.m. "Hi, Nana. It's great to see you," James swept his grandmother up in a big hug." I see you're all packed, so let's hit the road."

Chick loved this boy so much. Smart, funny, logical and focused on his education, James was everything one could hope for in a grandson. His younger brother Zach, was a sweetheart too, still in high school, still finding his path. There were seven years between them and Zach had always looked up to and emulated James, who teased him unmercifully as a child. Dahlia is an excellent mother and a great cook, but she didn't get it from me, Chick told others with a cheerful laugh. Privately, she felt in her heart of hearts that she herself had not been a good role model. Three husbands and a string of boyfriends had made Dahlia's childhood a roller coaster, a changing array of people and places. How could I have been so thoughtless, so naive? Chick chastised herself frequently, but one cannot change the past. She tried her best to be a good grandmother. Indeed, Dahlia didn't seem to blame her mother for her many past indiscretions, for which Chick was beyond grateful. Chick had a friend whose daughter would not communicate with her at all, cutting her off from her grandchildren, another acquaintance who was estranged from her son.

"But I was a great mother," wailed Carlie, when Chick confided her shortcomings in the parenting department. And yet her son would not speak to her. Truly heartbreaking. Chick felt she would drown in despair if she lost Dahlia.

James talked non-stop on the drive south about his escapades at Florida State, his girlfriend Brianna, his favorite classes and those he thought beyond lame, but were required. He shared his upcoming plans for graduate school at Southern Methodist University in Texas.

"Oh, James, I don't like the sound of that. Is it a religious school?"

"No, not at all, Nana. Southern Methodist has one of best lighting design program in the country, and they offer the best financial aid package around. It's nearly my dream scenario. And Brianna can come with me. She already has a job lined up," James said with a big smile.

The little chicken spent the weekend in the bosom of her family, surrounded with the love of her daughter and grandchildren. Unlike Chick, Dahlia was an accomplished homemaker and loved to entertain. Her home was spotless, the kitchen boasted every appliance and gadget she needed to prepare her signature lavish meals, served on the patio surrounding the swimming pool. Alas, Dahlia seemed to follow in Chick's footsteps regarding romantic partners. Here was yet another new boyfriend, CJ, a very friendly fellow who immediately called her Mom. That's okay. I like him, thought Chick. Maybe he's the one.

Chick retired to the guest room early. Though she felt loved, the truth was that at times being around her family made her feel ancient, like an artifact from a bygone era. And inept. Wasn't she supposed to be the crone archetype, channeling her inner wisdom, a diviner, a seeker, a prophetess? Not just an elderly technically challenged bird? She didn't know how to text, which seemed to be the latest thing. And she didn't have a smartphone, only a flip phone. Am I too dumb for a smartphone? she asked herself. Irritated and exasperated, she flopped down on the bed fully clothed. In Two-Lip around her friends, going out dancing, hanging out at the cafe, she felt vibrant, young, and yes, sexy.

Chick stared at the ceiling, covered with iridescent stars and planets, left over from when the boys were younger. Deep in thought and reaching a meditative state, she drifted into a dream. There she was in New York City, strolling in Times Square, wing in wing with a handsome stranger, dressed to kill, talking on her phone, when she suddenly stepped into a hole and felt herself falling, like Alice. It was not a rabbit hole, but a dark manhole, the blue sky a tiny receding circle above her. She tried in vain to grab a branch and. . . . Abruptly Chick awakened from her brief nightmare, perspiring and disoriented. As her thoughts cleared, she found within herself, a new resolve, a clarity of purpose. Yes, she absolutely would reinvent herself, start living up to her own expectations, get the latest smartphone and learn to text. She would buy a new laptop and start a blog. And yes, she'd buy that sequined dress she had her eye on and the fishnet stockings.

Bloody hell with aging gracefully.

14

A Fateful Meeting

Following the excitement and travel of the past few weeks, a sense of normalcy returned to Chick's peaceful life in the tiny burg of Two-Lip. On her busy schedule for this week was an organizational meeting of a new arts co-op. The group hoped to rent the beautiful old gothic church located right in the center of town. Chick was flattered that she, a fledgling artist, had been asked to be a founding member.

Thrilled and eager, she was the first to show up on Thursday morning. This venture could be a fantastic venue for the town, Chick hoped. What made it all so inspiring in the little chicken's mind was the building itself. A huge soaring space replete with stained glass, the light pouring through in a kaleidoscope of rainbow colors, and best of all, a magnificent polished hardwood floor, perfect for dancing. Would they let her be a booking agent for local bands? Though barely able to carry a tune herself, Chick loved music and singing, loved to dance, and fantasized about having a place to fulfill her dreams. She already had a rock and roll band in mind, the Relics out of Gainesville.

And Grant Peeples! The outspoken musician would be sure to shake up the local Republicans. The arty folks she was awaiting were mainly visual artists, but surely they would welcome artists of the musical variety, wouldn't they? Chick sat tapping her feet, lost in a daydream of fun-filled nights to come.

The days of our lives march on relentlessly into an unknown future. Pathos, joy, tragedy, a smorgasbord of wonderful and terrible things. This time, fate smiled down graciously upon the town and the people of Two-Lip. With countless hours of hard work, blood, sweat, and many tears, in only a few short months, an Artist Collective was born and grew to fruition. The group named the new venture Bananas, the former name of Two-Lip in days gone by. Chick's dream had come true.

On opening night, the double doors to Bananas swung wide open to an instant success. A shining disco ball, deafening rock music, vibrant and vivid art filled every available nook and cranny of the now deconsecrated church. The entire community seemed to have been waiting for a chance to break loose, to smile and laugh and dance. The crowd far exceeded the capacity for the room, Chick, worrier that she was, tried in vain to keep people from streaming in. She was not cut out to be a bouncer and eventually gave up. No one else seemed to care, the fire marshal be damned. He might have been inside dancing himself. It was Saturday night and upwards of a hundred folks were jammed into Bananas, gyrating, sweating, dancing with untamed energy to the Relics. The music was loud, the beer was flowing, and the air outside sweetened with reefer. The Three Sisters, benevolent spirits who reportedly haunted the old church were indeed pleased. Not a thing went wrong. People who Chick had never seen wearing anything but a frown, sported a big grin. She heard someone say, "It's a sixties mosh pit."

Chick danced her heart out, jumping for joy. She even danced with Turkey Lurkey. Who could have imagined the cranky old bird was such a good dancer?

The wonderful evening was drawing to a close when a handsome pearl gray cockatiel with a brilliant pink head-dress asked Chick for a dance. The song, Marvin Gaye's, Let's Get It On, filled the room as the two moved languorously across the floor, the beautiful bird whispering in her ear.

"I find you very attractive. I've been watching you all evening. Come and have a glass of wine with me. The moon is full and shining over Swan Lake."

Flustered, Chick stuttered, "Oh, I can't leave for hours. I have to help clean up this mess."

"That's okay, babe. The night is young and so are we," breathed the bird, her beak nibbling at Chick's ear. That's not precisely true, thought Chick, always acutely aware of her advancing age. Still, tonight she felt young, pretty and very hip. The bird continued to hold her close when the music ended.

"I know your name, you cute little chickpea. It's Chick. And mine is Theadora. My friends call me Teda. I want you to be my friend, my very special friend," the cockatiel said with a smile.

This bird is moving way too fast, Chick said to herself. And she's a female. Two-Lip was home to a sizable lesbian community, but she'd never seen Teda before. She'd have to ask her friend, Stormy, about her. And regardless, Chick was straight. Or was she? One would think she'd be quite certain of that at her age, but here she was, undeniably attracted to this lovely bird. Stormy had once told her it's never too late to explore one sexuality. Although Chick had attempted to flirt with lesbians she found appealing, it had never led to any encounters. If Chick was honest with herself and she usually was, she did fantasize about having a sexual encounter with another female. But could she fall in love with someone of the same sex? Chick simply didn't know. Feelings are fragile in love affairs. No one wants to be an experiment.

Still in the bird's embrace, these thoughts paraded through her head, a naked majorette with pink pom-poms leading the marching band.

Chick hesitated before answering, the proper little bird that she was, and shortly said, "Not this evening, but I'd love to meet for coffee one day soon, Theadora."

"I'd prefer tonight, but your wish is my command," the lovely bird said smoothly. "I'll be calling you, babe."

To Chick's delight and trepidation, her phone rang the next morning with an uncharacteristically insistent ring. Of course it was Teda.

15

A Chicken In Turkey

"How could I have fallen so hard so fast? Or maybe I don't know what love is." Chick glared into the bathroom mirror. "Surely, I'm not the fairest any longer nor the youngest. How could I have been so utterly stupid?" she asked the mirror, who, much like God, said nothing in return. Inspecting her beak for new signs of aging, she spied another gray feather amongst her eight thousand white feathers. "Yikes! I'm too young to go gray." Angrily, she plucked out the offending plumage.

"I need to start reading Pema Chodron again," she told her reflection. The inspiring words of the Buddhist nun had been a soothing influence in the past. "And meditate every day. I'll go out to the Temple of the Universe on Sunday and listen to Mickey Singer. I'm pathetic. I'm a mess!" she screeched. Chick was excellent at verbally beating herself up. But I have good reason to be upset, she rationalized. I thought Teda really loved me. And I loved her. I did. A tear slid down her cheek, and then another as Ms. Little let herself be sucked into going over once again, her sad story of love and loss, letting her mind revisit and analyze to the nth degree, the unhappy recent events. We all know the past cannot be changed, we know better than to dwell on the why and the what if of a heartbreak, and yet, like Chick, all too often we allow ourselves to get caught up in sorrow and are powerless to stop it.

The love story went like this . . .

When the phone rang the morning after the dance and it was Teda calling, Chick's heart did a flip-flop. I'd love to meet up, she'd said at once. From that day forward, in the blink of an eye, the two were inseparable. Theadora had money, real money, and she spent it freely, wining and dining Chick, like no one ever had. She was treated to weekends at the beach in a penthouse overlooking the Atlantic, dinners at chic restaurants, lavish gifts, (a diamond ankle bracelet) a rose every day for a week.

The lovestruck chicken's head was in the clouds, shimmering, silvery, soft and comfortable clouds. She'd never before been courted by a suitor with gobs of disposable income. It was fun. The rich are different. They have money. It was that simple. Chick was hooked. The love birds, (for a chicken is also a bird) spent hours gazing into each other's eyes. She felt incredibly close to Teda emotionally. Is it because she's a female, too? wondered Chick. To her amazement and delight, their love making was more than she could have ever imagined, carrying her to new heights of sexual ecstasy in a whirlwind of pure joy. Teda was inventive and a lover of sex toys. There was nothing she wouldn't try, all new to Chick, who only now realized what a conventional sex life she led previously. Chick would have married Teda if she'd asked, gone off to New York and tied the knot, where it had just become legal for same-sex couples to marry.

In a condo at the beach, the two lay in bed all day, rising only to eat and watch the sunset.

"Tell me more about your life, little chickadee. I want to know what you've done, where you've been. I want to know all about you," said Teda, wrapping her wings around Chick.

"Oh, you do? Well, I want to know more about you, mystery girl. I don't even know where you live," answered Chick.

"You first, babe," Teda said playfully

"All right, here goes. I made a parachute jump."

"What? No, I don't believe it!" exclaimed Teda, eyes wide.

"It's true," answered Chick. "So long ago now, they didn't do it in tandem like today. I did a static line jump, the line pulled open the parachute for you. I was the only female in a plane full of guys. They made me go first. If a woman can do it, then no man's going to want to look like a wimp. But I lost formation and screamed or so they told me. I think I passed out from fear," laughed Chick. "The chute opening jolted me back to consciousness. Floating down was truly gorgeous and breathtaking, not scary at all. Luckily I made a soft landing and didn't end up in a tree. Hey, Teda! Let's make a jump together. I've been thinking about another jump. Only two-hundred dollars, fifteen miles away in Palatka. It would be so much fun!"

Teda snorted. "Not me, baby, no way, not ever. Why would I jump out of a perfectly good airplane? That's a sweet story. What else? Tell me another one."

"Okay, I'm on a roll and you asked for it. I traveled to Turkey by myself. I was forty-nine years old and in the throes of a midlife crisis. Was I a wee bit crazy? Looking back, I would say yes. I flew by charter to Germany with plans to catch a direct bus into Istanbul, but I found out there was no bathroom on the bus. There was no way I was going to spend hours on a bus with no facilities, so I decided to take the train. It seemed like a good choice but turned out to be disastrous. I boarded the train in Munich and in the beginning it was lovely, clean and comfortable, nice people, beautiful views from the window . . . am I boring you? I can make a long story short," asked Chick suddenly. She wasn't really accustomed to talking this much about herself. No one usually asked her to.

"Chicky, I'm not a bit bored. I want to know and I'm dying to hear your tale. I'm hanging on your every word," Teda said teasingly, giving her a kiss on the toe. She had moved down to the end of the bed and was gently massaging Chick's feet.

She went on with her story. "So, there I was on the train, dozing off and on, munching my snacks, when it began to sink in how much my fellow passengers had changed. With every stop in the small towns, there were less families, less women, and more and more soldiers. When I ventured out to the bathroom, the halls were full of young men in uniform. I went back to my compartment, still occupied by myself and a family with children. But as the train slowed for the next station, they began to gather their belongings to exit the train. We had crossed the border into Yugoslavia. As we pulled into the town of Zagreb, there was a protest going on. A mob holding signs and shouting, police all around. I couldn't read the signs and I had no clue what was happening. The family got off, more and more soldiers got on, drinking, cursing, partying. They were on R&R, I found out later. Now, I was the only female in the car. I grabbed my backpack and went up and down the hall, searching for another woman, but it seemed like I was the only female. Most certainly the only chicken! The men either stared at me or ignored me. I thought, I'll go into the dining car, but it was the same there. All men. I sat down next to a young guy with a kind face and sort of clung to him until the dining car closed. He didn't speak English and I didn't speak Slovenian but I felt like he wanted to be my protector. He was small and slight, no match for the tall burly bullies. He tried to get me to return to his compartment with him, but I resisted. Did he just want to be the first to get into my pants? Was I going to get raped? I kept thinking how stupid I'd been to take the train. By now it was dark, nearly midnight. An announcement came on and I managed to understand that this train was at the end of the line in Belgrade, the capital. Serbia was called Yugoslavia at that time. It was a country in upheaval, on the brink of war, but I didn't know that. I stood by the door and when the train stopped, I was the first one off and I ran. I ran as fast as I could."

"Oh, Chick, you must have been terrified," said Teda, aghast.

"Yes, I was, but my ordeal was far from over. I ran through the station, out the front door to a line of taxis, picked the first one, jumped in and said take me to a hotel. I was shaking all over but I felt safe. For a minute. The taxi driver took off and kept going for blocks, passing what looked like hotels, and I kept saying hotel, hotel, in English of course. We were on a highway now. I thought I was being kidnapped. Many miles later the driver eventually pulled up to a small inn, stopped and helped me inside. I figured out later, he must have gotten a payment for bringing customers. Maybe it was his brother's establishment. That and the chance to collect on a long and expensive taxi ride. The hotel was creepy and weird, the desk clerk not friendly. I only had US dollars which he was reluctant to take. Finally, the clerk handed me a key and pointed at the elevator. More bad luck, it was room number thirteen. I shoved a chair under the doorknob and fell asleep." Chick felt shivery just retelling the sorry story all these years later.

"Now I'm in a hotel far from the city center with no guide book. I didn't speak a word of Serbo-Croatian. Remember, my itinerary was to take a through bus to Turkey. I'd never expected to be in Belgrade. The next day I managed to find a travel agent and I booked the first flight out. I was never getting on another train in my life. I spent a day on buses around the city but I seemed to be the only tourist. The funny thing is, it never even occurred to me to contact the American Embassy. I can be so clueless," said Chick, ruefully. "A day later, I flew into Turkey and everything turned around. I met great people to hang out with, went to a Turkish Bath. I bought a kilim. I ate Muslim bean pie. I went to Cappadocia and Ephesus. I had fun! But I can still say bed bugs in Turkish. Tahta kurusu. Oh, Teda, I could go on forever about my wonderful time in Turkey, but I'm done with talking. Now I want to hear about your adventures."

"Pretty amazing, Chick! I will say that was a story I hadn't expected, a truly hair-raising tale of woe. Frightening! I'm happy you survived to tell it. But me, now I'm more of a Club Med type. Give me a lounge chair, a pool, and a Mai Tai and I'm more than content," laughed Teda. "I do need a glass of wine after that scary saga."

Teda was in the kitchen pouring them both a glass of Pinot Noir, when her cell phone rang. Glancing at the display, she said, "I'll just take this outside, baby."

A good forty-five minutes went by with Teda still out on the balcony. Against her better judgment, Chick finally opened the sliding door, but Teda mouthed hush and motioned her back in. It must be a business call, she thought, and at that moment realized she had no idea what her lover did for a living. Teda had told her she was a consultant. She appeared to do nothing except spend money. Chick had asked around Two-Lip, but no one knew much if anything about her. In the two months (seven weeks and four days!) of being together the two had not socialized with Chick's friends. They'd gone to one dance at Bananas, but Teda wanted to leave nearly as soon as they arrived. Chick had never met any of Teda's friends or family. She'd been so caught up in their being together, being in love, she'd barely thought beyond the moment.

Teda came back into the room, saying, "Sorry, babe. just a few things needed solving. Let's drink up this wine and call it a night. I'm exhausted. And we need to get you back to Two-Lip in the morning." The two birds had been staying at a Fernandina beach condo overlooking the white sandy beaches of the Atlantic.

"But I thought we were staying all week," said Chick, puzzled at the change of plans.

"You thought wrong, Ms. Little. Let's go to sleep." Shortly, Teda was snoring. Chick's eyes stayed wide open well past 2:00 a.m.

Everything seemed back to normal in the morning. Teda kissed Chick gently until she woke up, a hot cup of coffee waiting for her. On the drive home, Chick sat up close to Teda, ignoring the seatbelt in favor of cuddling. They stopped at a roadside stand for boiled peanuts and sat in the shade feeding them to each other like the lovebirds they were.

A long kiss goodbye at Chick's door and the idyllic days came to an end.

"It was fun, Chicky. We had a blast. Don't call me, I'll call you," said Teda, as she got into the car, something she had never said before. Chick put it out of her mind.

16

Reality Dawns At Sunset

Two entire days passed with no call from Teda. They had always talked every day and on the few days the two hadn't seen each other, spent hours on the phone. On the morning of the third day, Chick, in a moment of weakness, dialed Teda's number. It went straight to voicemail. She didn't leave a message. Chick was bewildered.

"Does she need some space? But gee, we could have talked about it," Chick said out loud. She was beginning to feel a very unpleasant knot of anxiety building in the pit of her stomach. Had she talked too much? Not enough? Halitosis? She knew something was very wrong but wouldn't quite give free reign to her misgivings.

The next day, Teda called.

"Sorry, babe, I want to see you but it'll have to be Saturday, maybe Sunday," she said brusquely.

"Oh, what happened? Is it your job? Or a problem with your family?" Chick asked naively.

"You could say that and you did," Teda answered with a bark of a laugh. "Don't push me, babe. I don't like being questioned. I said I'd call and I will. Again." Teda answered in a tone of voice Chick had never heard her use before. It wasn't a pretty sound.

Chick didn't. Push her, that is. Alone, she spent hours cleaning her house, working outside in the yard, yanking angrily at the proliferation of air potatoes that could easily engulf her property, hacking away at the unrelenting greenery that was Florida. Chick got back to her last painting, half finished and neglected along with everything and everyone since meeting Teda. With a steadily sinking heart, she indulged in endless speculation over what exactly was going on. One thing she did not do was phone Goosey, who had already voiced her disapproval with the speed of the affair.

"It's not that she's a female. Why, I could see myself falling for a bird like Teda," Goosey had said to Chick's surprise, during one of the few times she'd even talked with her friend in the last month. "She reminds me of k.d. Lang," Goosey said dreamily. This made no sense as Teda looked nothing like k.d. Nor did Teda look like Wayne Newton, whom k.d. had come to resemble, in Chick's opinion. A lot of straight women had a crush on the singer, mused Chick. She admired the woman for her stance against meat consumption, regardless of the detrimental effects to her musical career. After seeing her sexy and funny performance at Disney World, dancing in a tutu, and then discarding it, Chick was infatuated too.

Sunday evening at 7:00 p.m. when Chick had given up hope of Teda calling by the weekend and was ready to call her again, even though she promised herself she would not, the phone rang.

"Meet me at the Bay in twenty minutes," Teda said abruptly.

She must think I'm sitting by the phone waiting for a call, thought Chick, though she most certainly was. Shortly, despite her wounded ego, there she was seated across from Teda (not side by side) in a back booth of the Bay.

"Please. Tell me what's happening, Teda," Chick said, feeling queasy. She could almost see her heart on her sleeve.

"Look, babe. I'm sorry. It's over between us. I'm married, Chick. My wife's been out of the country and now she's returned. Yes, we've been estranged and I thought we were headed for divorce court, but we're going to give it another try. Believe me, I do care for you, Chick," Teda said softly.

And just like that, the affair ended. Chick's rose colored glasses slipped off her beak, fell to the floor and shattered into a thousand pieces of pain and betrayal.

She ran from the restaurant in tears.

17

Across The Pond

Life is weird. Life is strange. Life is a bitch. Chick's little heart was indeed broken, but it would mend and she would be stronger and wiser, she vowed. She would be like Superchicken and not let this experience make her bitter. Teda was a deceitful and beguiling bird, a master at lies of omission. Even her feathers were dyed (Chick had found a bottle of pink dye in the medicine chest). She decided not to tell her daughter about the short lived affair. How many times had Dahlia seen Chick fall in love? And out of love? She'd just tell me to grow up, thought Chick.

It is often said that time heals, or at the least, time makes the wound less raw. Chick had picked up her broken heart and with duct tape and super glue, put it back together. Her art, her friends, her re-energized activism (she'd gotten involved in a battle to keep a sturgeon farm out of Two-Lip) and her work at Bananas all kept her from drowning in a well of self-pity. If Chick had learned anything from the disastrous affair, it was that if one were to label her sexual orientation, she was a bisexual bird.

"I never thought I could fall in romantic love with another female," she told Goosey one evening over a glass of wine. "But I could and I did. Love is love." She wondered if it would ever happen again. Chick had thought this relationship would be easier than with a man, but it wasn't. Not at all.

Spring had sprung in north central Florida. The azaleas were blooming, the dogwoods were flowering, and the spiders were hatching. Two big wolf spiders in the bathroom this morning and a roach in her underwear drawer were an unwelcome surprise. With a shriek, she tried to smash the nearest arachnid with a book, to no avail. So much for ahimsa, she thought contritely. The philosophy of nonviolence, of non-killing, was far more difficult to practice with creatures perceived as unpleasant, creepy, or dangerous, even if they were harmless. Humid subtropical Two-Lip, Florida was teeming with all manner of insects. Chick's benevolence was tested daily.

True to her promise, Precious had invited her to come to Wales. The invitation came with very short notice, but Chick was delighted. And it was a chance to put some distance between herself and the scene of her recent heartache. She was to fly out of Gainesville next Monday, or on the Monday, as Precious would say. They spoke the same language, English, but there were so many different ways of saying things, as Chick was to learn.

Ms. Little was in a tizzy about what to pack. Should she go for a casual comfortable look? Or a sophisticated woman of the world? What do chickens wear in London? She set off for the church dollar-a-bag sale, the source of the majority of her wardrobe. Nevertheless, her friends frequently complimented her on her choice of clothing.

"Just look at you!" said Reed, a fellow artist she'd run into at the last Art Walk. Chick loved to mix patterns. That evening she was decked out in a yellow azo and lime green flowered skirt, a lemony checked blouse, strings of dichroic multi-colored glass beads, cobalt blue and green shoes, carrying a shiny red bag. "I'll bet even your undies match," Reed said with a wink. Chick colored and rolled her eyes. He was right, her knickers were red.

"I'll be a fashionista!" she clucked, home from the sale, in her bedroom, trying on a new black fleece jacket with the price tag still attached. It fit her perfectly. A pair of black jeans, black and white striped tee shirt and a yellow print scarf completed the ensemble.

"I look smokin' hot," exclaimed Chick to the mirror. Should she need different clothes while in Britain, Precious had assured her there were plenty of charity shops as thrift stores were called in the UK. And she could borrow from Precious. Not surprisingly, the sisters were exactly the same size.

Opting to scale down, Chick stood ready and waiting with her carry-on suitcase in front of her house on the Monday. Stormy had readily agreed to drive her the short distance to the airport.

"You look fantastic," enthused her friend. "Very continental. You go, girl!"

"Ciao, Stormy. Thanks so much for the lift." Chick waved goodbye, and with a flourish, she was off on yet another Big Adventure.

The chicken dozed fitfully throughout the long flight, unable to concentrate on a movie or read a book. She was thoroughly disgusted by the man across the aisle, who kept loudly blowing his nose and tossing the used tissues on the floor. Some people. Bleary-eyed as she trudged through customs, the agent was unsympathetic and downright rude, implying she would stay beyond her allotted six months, and asking to see her return trip ticket before letting her pass.

"If I were young and blonde, I'll bet he wouldn't have been such a dick," fumed Chick under her breath. "And taller."

There at long last was her beautiful sister, Precious, so excited to see her that she ducked under the cord meant to keep people back and enveloped her in a big hug. In the US, she'd well have been detained for such an action, but apparently not in Britain.

"I've planned masses of things for us to do, lovey! But first we need food." They piled into the car, an electric VW. Chick was jealous, positively green with envy. Precious could drive. Of course, here in the UK, the steering wheel was on the right side and one drove in the left lane, causing Chick's heart to leap to her throat more than once. They stopped at a caff (cafe) for brekkie (breakfast) where Chick ordered oatmeal and toast. Yuck. It's difficult to ruin such simple fare, but the Brits are renowned for bland food. The meal was fairly awful, the coffee weak. Chick bit her tongue as Precious didn't seem to notice, wolfing down her food with gusto.

"It's nearly two hours to home, Chick. Doze off if you like. I well know what jet lag feels like."

"Oh, I couldn't. I want to see the countryside," Chick intoned as her eyelids drooped, sound asleep in a matter of seconds. She woke with a start when Precious stopped the car in front of a picturesque cottage set in rolling hills dotted with sheep, and a garden overflowing with roses, peonies, hollyhocks, tomatoes, squash, and cucumbers, all mixed together in a formal yet wild looking jumble.

"My garden does tend to get a wee bit overgrown. I must get to it straightaway," laughed Precious. "Come now. Alfred is so anxious to meet you."

"Welcome to our family, Chick," Alfred embraced her warmly. He was a handsome man appearing far younger than his seventy-two years. "Get settled in. I'll go down to our wine cellar and bring up a bottle I've been saving for just such a momentous occasion as this."

The cottage adjoined an ancient church and graveyard,

which Chick did find a bit unsettling. Her window from the guest room afforded a view of the crumbling gravestones. Looking down on the neatly manicured lawn, Chick resolved once again to live her remaining years to the fullest, to be present in the moment and stay positive. She knew it wouldn't be long before she'd be joining those folks underground.

Staying happy and upbeat wasn't hard to do here in Wales with her charming hosts. Precious and Alfred delighted in showing her the sights daily, a walk across the Monmouth Bridge and Gate, hiking the Bourne Woods, a visit to a country craft fair where Chick found a unique bag constructed of hemp. She intended to leave the bag as a surprise gift for her sister, whose current purse was unraveling at the seams. A highlight was a day trip to the Hay Festival, a prestigious book fair where they were privileged to hear a talk by a favorite author of both the sisters, Jeanette Wilkerson. They missed getting a ticket to hear Salman Rushdie. Still, it was a privilege to be in close proximity to world-renowned authors.

Exploring castles had always been a favorite family activity. They toured so many, Chick lost count. Raglan Castle was a short distance from the house, a 15th century late medieval specimen that Precious and her children spent many enjoyable hours in over the years, the boys delighting in stabbing each other with fake swords. It seems there were ruins of a castle on every corner, some in near pristine condition. Searching out quaint pubs was another family pursuit. One evening the trio had dinner in a working class pub in downtown Monmouth. Chick drank two huge steins of beer and became quite silly and woozy, a single bottle being her usual limit.

"I'll just visit the loo," she said daintily, where she proceeded to get sick. Perhaps it was the stuffed mushrooms. What were they stuffed with? She regretted not asking.

Her stomach was doing flip flops. So much strange food, bland though it was, didn't always agree with her digestive system, which had become quite finicky of late.

On the weekend the three took the train into London. Chick was beyond thrilled to ride a double-decker bus through Trafalgar Square, visit the Tower of London, standing in awe as Big Ben chimed in the distance.

The only disappointment of the day was that the rest of the family were not in London at the moment.

"I'm so sorry that Sally and the boys, too, are out of town just when you're visiting. That was totally unexpected and simply bad timing. Next time you come overseas, we'll have a big party, a real family reunion," said Precious, lovingly.

"And there will be a next time," Alfred chimed in. "You're a delight, Chick. I'm so pleased for both of you."

Next on the day's itinerary was the Tate Modern. They had just missed the Diego Rivera exhibit, but were in time to see Monet. To be truthful, Chick would have preferred to see the work of Frida Kahlo. She would have liked to see more of any woman's work. Chick was filled with outrage that so few of the artworks in the vast space were done by women. This was true of all the major museums Chick had visited, in Washington, D.C., Boston, even Prague in the Czech Republic. Women were underrepresented.

"It's no wonder we had to open our own museum, the National Museum of Women in the Arts in D.C., " Chick told her sister. "An afternoon there will open your eyes." The inequitable situation made her blood boil. She remembered her visit to a small private art museum in Alabama where they displayed one lonely drawing by a female artist, Mary Cassatt, hung in, of all places, the bathroom. For shame! Things would improve somewhat in the coming years, but in 2015, the Tate Modern had granted women artists solo exhibitions only twenty-five per cent of the time since 2007. Equality in the arts had a long road ahead. Chick had been looking forward to seeing the new Tracy Emin exhibit but they had run out of time. Chick admired Emin immensely. Now there was an artist who had made a name for herself in the art world, who said and did what she wanted to, however outrageous or controversial. Good for her!

Chick did love London. The little family had a delightful outing, even whilst getting caught in a downpour without a brolly (umbrella). They had to literally run to catch the last train back to the countryside. The visit to the Capitol had been brilliant, a day to remember.

With only a few days remaining of her visit, she and Precious left the next morning for a drive to the Jurassic Coast of England to visit Shelly, a lifelong friend of Precious. She and her husband, Byron, lived in an amazing house, perched precariously on a hill overlooking the sea. Thrilled for her dear old friend's good fortune, Shelly welcomed Chick warmly into the fold, showing her to the guest room, a tiny loft with a cupola, a view of the ocean stretching for miles in either direction. The day was chilly and foggy, the norm for England. Bundled up, they all strolled on Chesil Beach, famous for fossils. Chick loaded her pockets while knowing she could take only a few home with her. Each one was so fascinating! Unique souvenirs, she reasoned, and free. Dorset was lined with small villages, postcard perfect, a mecca for artists. I could live here, she thought. She felt that about every place she liked. If only it weren't so very expensive. Her dollar didn't stretch far in the UK, especially compared to Mexico. If she wanted to live in a foreign country, it wouldn't be here. Always on the lookout for a possible locale to realize her dream of living as an expat, her research had shown Albania to be comparatively cheap for Europe. Chick didn't know a word of Albanian. Was she too old to learn?

No visit to the Dorset Coast was complete without a stop at the Abbotsbury Swannery. Whoever knew there were so many of the gorgeous graceful birds in need of rescue? Chick was mesmerized. She'd never been up close to a swan and there were hundreds of them. They wouldn't leave her alone, especially a large black one who kept plucking at her tail feathers. She finally had to go indoors. Apparently the swans had never before had a chicken visitor.

The sole disconcerting aspect of the visit to Shelly and Byron's home was the gigantic dog that lived with them. Precious had no fear at all of the dog, aptly named Brutus, but Chick was wary of dogs, especially large ones, and the dog could sense it. After a lovely dinner and an evening chat on the patio, they all said good night. Once again, Chick drank too much wine. She had only herself to blame, yes, but her hosts kept refilling her empty glass and it went down ever so smoothly. She could have said no. All the wine found her getting up from her bed again shortly to relieve herself. Her room was at the opposite end of the house from the bathroom and Chick padded down the hall, the canine terror completely forgotten. She had just shut the bathroom door when she realized Brutus had been right behind her. Now she could hear the dog snorting and breathing under the door. To make matters worse, there was no loo paper. The roll was empty. She was forced to use the bidet, no small feat for a short little chicken. Her business finished, she was afraid to open the door. Oh dear, will I have to spend the night in here? she said to herself. Or shall I start yelling and wake up the whole household? She nearly burst into tears. No matter that Shelly had assured her that Brutus was harmless. Ms. Little was terrified.

Feel the fear and walk through it, she told herself. It took her a good twenty minutes but she gathered her courage and opened the door. The dog wasn't there. She flew down the hall (not literally, although we know she is a bird). Quickly closing the door to her room, she breathed a sigh of relief and . . . awk! There was a large dark form smack in the middle of her bed. Brutus. Brutus was in her bed!

"Oh, help!! Help!" The chicken stood frozen, her voice only a tiny squeak. In the semi-darkness, she could see the dog had one eye open. He didn't move and neither did she. One moment stretched into a thousand. Wait a minute. What was that thumping noise? Was that his tail? Was Brutus wagging his tail?

"Nice doggy. Good dog." Chick said tentatively. His tail thumped harder. "Could you get down, please? Brutus? Pretty please? Please get down."

"Down, boy, down," said Chick in a somewhat stern tone. Obediently, the dog jumped off the bed and curled up on the rug. Quite astonished at the turn of events, Chick gave the dog a pat on the head and happily climbed back into bed.

"Oh, jeepers creepers," said Chick, words she had never used before popped into her head and out of her mouth unbidden. She had no idea where they came from.

We all have our stories we like to retell. The Night of the Sleeping Dog would become a favorite of the brave little chicken. In her version, she was not nearly as much of a wuss and Brutus was much bigger and meaner.

18

Freedom On Wheels

Another sad goodbye was in store for the newly reunited sisters. Amidst many tearful hugs, they resolved to get together again as soon as they possibly could. As in all major airports, long gone were the days when your loved ones could accompany you to the gate and watch you board the plane, and Heathrow was no exception. Chick, too prideful to request assistance, walked and walked trailing her luggage, finally arriving exhausted at her gate, just in time to queue up for boarding.

Finding her sister was still all so amazing and wonderful, Chick reflected as she gazed out from her window seat far above the clouds. She was most grateful that her seatmate kept her nose buried in a book. Chick didn't feel like small talk or any talk. She blew up her inflatable pillow, put it around her neck, her jacket over her legs, and promptly fell asleep.

The return trip was thankfully uneventful, no delays, no missed connections. In no time at all, her European trip was over and there she was, home in her sweet little cottage, jet lagged once again and happy to be back. She had barely put her luggage down when her phone crowed like a rooster, a most comforting sound. It was her faithful friend, Goosey.

Without preliminaries, Goosey launched right into her news. "Chick! Guess what? Wait until you hear this. Ford just came out with a new car. The SmarterCar! Anyone can drive it. No height restrictions. Outfitted for all types of disabilities," said Goosey, reading the ad. "You can have a car, Chick!"

"Oh! Oh. Oh, my God, really? Is it really true? What if I can't pass the driving test? Can I afford one? Oh, it sounds too good to be true," said the little chicken, ever the pessimist.

"It's absolutely true, Chick. I'll teach you to drive myself. You have some savings, I know you do. Put some money down and make payments. Look, call John at Santa Fe Ford and give him my name. He'll get you the best possible deal. I've got it all figured out," finished up Goosey. "This is going to change your life!"

You can teach an old chicken new tricks. Chick learned to drive for the first time, well into her sixties. On the right side of the road. She would never drive in Britain, of that she was adamant. Thanks to Goosey, whose patience was boundless, Chick passed her driving test with flying colors, blue, magenta, red, and turquoise, her favorites. A bit over a month later, John handed Chick the keys to her brand new SmarterCar. The car was a mustard yellow with a black stripe. She couldn't resist a vanity plate. FRE CHIC. And she was. A free chicken. It was a dream come true. Oh, the glorious freedom! After a lifetime of public transportation and depending on others, she was an independent bird. Chick named her new car Fancy Free. Fancy for short. Ms. Little was over the moon with happiness.

Her daughter was a bit less enthusiastic. "Mom, you always seem so nervous riding in the car. You're the world's worst backseat driver. Are you sure you can drive? On I-75?" asked Dahlia.

"Honey, I passed my driver's test, didn't I? The State of Florida gave me a license," said Chick indignantly. "Don't worry so much."

"Alrighty, then. If you're sure, come down and visit us soon. Just be extra careful. And watch out for the semi trucks. And left turns. Your car is so tiny and so are you. We love you and we all want you around for a long time." Her daughter sounded stressed. She's more of a worrywart than I am, thought Chick as she ended the call.

Goosey was correct. Chick's life had radically changed. How exhilarating it was! Why, she could go anywhere at any time she damn well pleased. And she did. She drove into Gainesville and went to Wards, to Publix, to the Repurpose Project, the Hippodrome, the current art exhibit at the Thomas Center. She totally surprised her old friend, Carole, popping in unexpectedly.

"You could take a road trip, Chick. Your car gets such good gas mileage. I'd love to go off on a journey, but I simply don't have the gumption. I get nervous just driving out to Two-Lip," Carole said wistfully.

The seed was planted. By the time Chick turned smartly into her driveway, she had mapped out in her mind an Odyssey worthy of Homer.

"I'll visit everyone I know. I'll camp at state parks, I'll go to Buffalo and Michigan and Oregon, down to Mexico and Austin and . . . ," Chick said out loud, all in a rush. Talking to herself would become a habit, especially while driving. Singing too. But not with passengers present. She was well aware of her terrible voice, flat, squeaky, and scratchy. No matter, the chicken still loved to sing.

Once Chick hatched an idea, she didn't easily give it up. This dream trip would come to fruition, she was positive of that.

In the meantime, she was thoroughly enjoying her newfound independence. Happy to repay in kind, at least some of the errands her pals had helped her with over the years, she proudly transported her friends to Hawthorne for lunch, to Palatka for concerts, to the local farmer's markets. Everyone loved her SmarterCar.

"I want one!" was the common refrain, especially among other fowl. This car had opened up a whole new world for anyone of short stature, for anyone with wings. Ducky was the friend who had benefited the most. He tooled around town in his very first car, a bright orange convertible, sporting a huge grin, and waving at everyone. Chick still couldn't quite believe the good fortune this marvel of technology had brought into her life and the lives of countless others, human and animal alike. If she was ever lucky enough to meet the inventor of her car, she would bow down and kiss her feet. Or his feet.

"I'd better do a few camping practice runs before my big trip. Get my gear in order," Chick told Ducky. She and Goosey had driven over to Cedar Key, thinking it would be a nice place to try for a first outing, but the no-see-ums were relentless. Quite unstoppable, they came right through the screens she had fitted to her front windows. Even Chick's feathers were no match for the voracious insects.

She opted for a trip to the beach instead. Chick called her friend, Stormy, who took off frequently for the sandy shores. Chick had always envied her. And now she could drive herself!

"They might hassle you for sleeping in your car at the state park," Stormy warned her. "It's an outrage. Camping isn't only for the rich. My station wagon is my camping unit. If they don't like it, tough." Stormy knew her rights.

Her tiny car packed to the roof with more supplies than she could use in a month, Chick set off for Anastasia State Park. Like the good Girl Scout she once was, this chicken liked to be prepared. She had no reservation, but her good luck held, as she snagged the last available campsite, very private and under a shady tree. Checking in, no one questioned her sleeping arrangements. To be sure to avoid any confrontation, she put up her pup tent. Why chance an unpleasant encounter? And the tent came in handy for storing extra goods.

Paradise! The little bird sat back in her comfy camp chair, feet up, drinking an icy cold beer. This was her idea of heaven. The sun set over the treetops, turning the azure blue skies to lavender and hot pink. Seagulls called out in the distance. She'd spotted a roseate spoonbill on the drive to her site, and a blue heron stalking a fiddler crab in the marsh. All was not yet lost. There was still a glimmer of hope for the survival of the natural world.

As darkness fell, it dawned on Chick that she was quite alone. Although she lived alone, when she went out, it was always with at least one buddy. This would all be a new experience. A vehicle gives you freedom, but it can also isolate you, she pondered. Surviving solo, being on the road as a single female, with its myriad possibilities for trouble, flat tires, overheating, wiper blades flying off, strange guys giving you the once over could be a challenge. She'd been through plenty of this with her pals over her lifetime. But her car was brand spanking new, not prone to sudden breakdowns, she reasoned. And she had purchased AAA extended service, just to be on the safe side.

"I can do this. I'm a strong old bird. I'm Superchicken. I'll be just fine," she said to the trees. Flashlight in hand or rather in wing, she made her way down the brushy path to the bathrooms, where she chatted up a woman from Nova Scotia who was doing her laundry, and with that simple exchange, quelled her feelings of loneliness. Back at her campsite, she lit a small fire, enjoyed her dessert first, heated up a can of beans and ate them right out of the can. Spinach salad and tofu in peanut sauce brought from home topped off the delicious dinner. Snug in her made-to-order sleeping bag and memory foam mattress, she slept soundly, waking at dawn. The flowered curtains she'd made for the car needed a little tweaking to keep out the morning sun, the coffee makings were buried under everything, but overall the arrangement was quite comfy.

In the early morning, Chick walked to the beach. The wind off the ocean blew her feathers straight back as she stood at the water's edge, the waves lapping at her feet.

"My life is good. I'm so very grateful for my new freedom and for all that I have," she whispered to the universe. The little chicken and her feathered friends in Two-Lip had already lived far beyond their life expectancy, another phenomena that science could not explain. Chick had every reason to be filled with gratitude.

19

Things Are Bigger In Texas

As has been mentioned before, Chick was no spring chicken. She could glimpse old age on the horizon, closing in fast. With that image in mind, she'd finalized her plans for her Big Adventure in record time. No grass was going to grow under her feet, Chick had resolved. She took the old adage quite literally. Her yard was a Florida xeriscape with edible plants, bromeliads, native grasses and ground cover, stone walkways, and a lily pond. She had no worries of her non-existent lawn turning brown in a drought. Her place needed little upkeep. Lucky for Chick, since she'd gotten wheels, she was rarely at home. Last weekend, she braved the four hour trip on the interstate to Sarasota to visit Dahlia. Her family was proud of her, they told her, and considerably impressed by her and her car. With relish, she described in detail her upcoming travel plans. Far from being discouraging, all were excited for her and wished her well.

"Yes, do it while you still can. One of these days I just might go with you, Mom," said Dahlia. "You can drive me around for a change."

Back at the Bay in Two-Lip, Chick met Goosey, Henny, Ducky, and Turkey for a farewell drink. Our intrepid chicken was off on what could be the grandest adventure of her life. It wasn't. Chick was destined to have even more grandiose experiences in the coming years, but she did not yet know that.

The old friends raised their glasses in a toast. "To Chick, may you have blue skies and green lights, my friend. I'll miss you so much," said Goosey, gazing mournfully at her dear friend.

"That's a good one!" chuckled Ducky. "Absolutely no red lights and no po-po. Keep within the speed limit and don't fall asleep at the wheel. Chew on sunflower seeds. All that crunching will keep you awake."

Turkey took a big swig of the house red and raised his glass high. "Wherever you go, there you are, my dear," said the old bird, ever the cynic. "You may find that everything you search for is right here."

Only Henny was strangely quiet, saying, "Be safe out there. It's dangerous." Yes, Henny had surely changed of late, though she assured her friends she was fine. The hen used to be enthusiastic and up for anything. Now she was subdued and always seemed distracted. Everyone was a bit worried about her.

Sunday at 8:00 a.m. saw Chick well on her way, her trusted GPS set for points west. A Bonnie Raitt CD blasting from the speakers, she blew a kiss to Clark as her car breezed through the only stoplight in town (green) the open road stretched out before her.

"I'm free! Free as a bird," she screeched, missing the inherent irony in her proclamation. No one to answer to, enough money to last for the foreseeable future, and except for her promise to Goosey not to go to Slab City, beholden to no one. As the miles slid by, she considered again the offer extended to her by her friend, Hope. If Chick would agree to arrive in Austin by mid-December, she could have a house-sitting gig. Much as she was intrigued by the idea of no fixed itinerary, the enticing possibility of a stay in a cute vintage trailer in downtown Austin began to sound appealing. Set in the heart of the music scene, Hope had told her she could even walk to the river and to Whole Foods, better known as whole paycheck. That she knew no one in town and might possibly spend Christmas alone didn't faze her. She could paint, listen to live music, visit the food trucks, haunt the thrift shops and go rummaging through Goodwill-By-The-Pound. Yes, Chick decided, she'd head for Austin, a music mecca she'd long dreamed of visiting, a bastion of liberal thinking in a deep red state, a city of almost a million people. That it was once a sister city of Gainesville was unthinkable now.

Three grueling days later, Chick pulled into a gas station for a pit stop and to call Hope. She had not made good time on the road. This was her first long interstate trip where she was the driver and she found the congestion and endless construction on I-10 horrific. Her SmarterCar was dwarfed by the gigantic trucks and it seemed as if everyone drove well above the speed limit. And she would have to rethink her camping situation. Sleeping in the back of her car might not work out after all. It was frigid the first night in Alabama at a state park and although she paid for electricity to plug in her heater, she couldn't get it to work. The other campers had stared at her. She wasn't sure if it was because she was a solo chicken or that her rig didn't measure up to their behemoth Class A RVs and Fifth Wheels. They're probably Republicans, she thought, disgruntled, and true, she spotted two McCain bumper stickers on the way to the bathhouse. At the end of her rope, she hadn't even taken a shower once she found a site. The last straw was . . . 'I Support the Second Amendment' sticker slapped on the bathroom mirror.

"Get over it!" she said loudly, her voice an echo in the empty bathroom. Chick was overjoyed that Obama had been re-elected. The right of fowls like herself to vote was being challenged yet again. She was totally disenchanted with the political circus in America, the provincial attitudes, the way the country was so divided, the endless forever wars across the globe. A sign she had seen in Tallahassee proclaimed . . . 'Earth: The Insane Asylum of the Universe'. If you were an alien being from a peaceful planet, would you stop here? Chick thought not. She frequently felt like an outsider in this crazy world. And her avid interest in politics had waned. She knew decisions were made that affected people's lives, but she could no longer take it so seriously. Her absentee ballots couldn't catch up with her, but she was nearly beyond caring. Ms. Little would live by her own principles. That would have to be enough.

When her time in Austin was over, she planned to head for Mexico after the first of the year, where she had a standing invitation to stay with her long time friends, Aaron and Emilio, in the town of Alamos. Chick still harbored a fantasy of living out her remaining years as an expat in an exotic locale. Her meager savings could stretch so much further, an important point for a geriatric chicken.

"Whew! I'm lucky it's Sunday." Chick whipped across four lanes of little traffic to get off at the Lamar exit in South Austin. She was right on time to meet Hope for brunch at Maria's Taco Express and Hippie Church. Sounds cool, she had said to Hope, for if she were to again label herself, it would be aging hippie. The word 'church' did put her off a bit, but she trusted her friend's recommendation. Swinging into the parking lot under a giant statue of what looked to be a woman in Purgatory holding a bouquet of flowers, surrounded by beatific putti, those winged infant angelic spirits, and bright red grinning devils, she had second thoughts. Is it a church after all? she asked herself.

One couldn't tell from the exterior. Opening the carved wooden doors, she ran straight into Hope.

"Girlfriend!!" they both said in unison. "So wonderful to see you again, Hope," gushed Chick. "It's been, what? Three years since you came to Florida? Far too long."

Hope was one of her favorite people on the planet. Chick so admired her friend's boundless creative energy and her hilarious tales of her world travels. Hope blew her own glass beads, turning them into gorgeous jewelry, selling her wares in the summer at craft fairs all over the south and northeast. An avid dancer, she wintered in Texas, relaxing and soaking in all that Austin had to offer.

Chick was ravenous and the wait in the long line was worth it. Bean and potato tacos for two dollars each. She ate four and could have eaten another. Hope, rail thin, was still finishing up one. Chick suddenly felt like a glutton.

"Let's dance!" squawked Chick, as the gospel group cranked up with an irresistible rockin' beat.

"Not me. Remember I'm into swing and the Texas two-step, not this unstructured stuff." Hope pulled out her knitting and put in her ear plugs.

"Oh, I forgot." Chick bounced in her seat, feet tapping. She was reluctant to get up there alone but obviously her friend wasn't going to budge. Chick would have to dance on a table top like a stripper lest she be trampled. Dance while you can . . . her favorite motto waltzed through her head and she couldn't resist. Jumping up, she headed for the dance floor.

This was a good thing. A very good thing. Chick boogie-woogied straight into the wings of the most handsome turkey she'd ever laid eyes on. We will not say it was love at first sight, we won't even think about it. The dazzling turkey exuded a passionate sensuality mixed with loving kindness that sucked the little chicken in like quicksand. Turkey Lurkey back in Two-Lip was considered handsome, but his abrasive and arrogant personality could make him downright ugly in Chick's opinion. This turkey was a sweetie and an excellent dancer.

Too bad his name is Tom, she did say to herself. Tom Turkey. Come on. Spare me. Yet she couldn't deny that her heart was making that all too familiar pitter-patter sound. She felt positively giddy. And sticky and sweaty. She desperately needed a shower.

"Wow! Unbelievable," said Hope later, back at her trailer. "You've only been in Austin a few hours and you've already got a date." Tom had asked her to meet for breakfast in the morning.

"It's just coffee. He wants to pick my brain about kayaking in north Florida next spring. It's not a real date," stammered Chick. But in her fickle little heart, she knew it was.

In a few days, Hope had departed for Michigan and Chick had fallen hard for both Tom Turkey and the city of Austin. She spent every spare minute with the handsome bird. Chick was thrilled to find that Tom sang, played guitar, and even had a Tuesday afternoon gig at the Continental Club. There she was hanging out with a performer! How lucky could one chicken be? He introduced her to ecstatic dance, a freeform movement, a dance done with no inhibitions, a dance one could feel deeply within your whole being. This was the way Chick always danced, but she'd never danced wordlessly in a vast room with seventy-five other souls, moving to beautiful music that built to a crescendo transporting one to other realms. You could touch other dancers if they were receptive. Some people became intertwined in twos or threes or more, knots on the floor. It was very sensual, yet highly respectful of another's personal space. The dance flowed sublime and nonverbal, ending in a circle of sharing and connection, holding hands. Some people cried. Other people shared their innermost thoughts. It was like nothing Chick had ever before experienced. Already she was planning to start this moving meditative dance at Bananas back in Two-Lip.

Ten days later, Hope returned as scheduled, and our chicken's house-sit came to an end. They had quickly realized the tiny trailer would not accommodate two. When Chick knocked one of Hope's new glass pieces to the floor and spilled coffee on her grandmother's vintage quilt, she could read the writing on the wall. It said, 'it's time for you to go.' And it was also time to say goodbye to Tom. They had both realized their brief affair was little more than a fling. The two birds would remain friends in the years ahead, until Tom died of a heart attack, far too young, at fifty-three.

Chick's tentative plan was to drive south to San Antonio. Clark had a cousin with a ten acre farm outside of town. She was welcome to visit and even leave her car with him if she decided not to drive to Mexico. She'd been dragging her heels about the best way to make her way to the town of Alamos, five hundred miles below the border and off the beaten path. Located much too near the dangerous state of Sinaloa, Sonora wasn't much safer. The nearest airport was fairly close by in Obregon but the flight was outrageously expensive. From there she would still have to catch a bus to Alamos. Or she could take a first class bus from Tucson, but she'd not been able to obtain the dreaded tourist card. The lone chicken would have to get it at the border and brave the stop and go passenger screening light. Admittedly, she was afraid to drive, but leery of taking the bus. This quandary refused to resolve itself and left her in limbo.

Saying farewell to Hope, Chick hopped in her car for the hour and a half drive to San Antonio. Now she was seated in a comfortable rocking chair on the front porch of Tony's log cabin, having a beer with her new friend.

"Would the goddess guide me to a decision if I truly

believed in her powers of intervention?" Chick asked Clark's cousin. She'd read that three in ten adults in the US felt that God influenced the outcome of sporting events. Apparently their God cared more about football than children starving in Yemen. She, he, or it, neither cares nor has a hand in our fate, in Chick's opinion. We're on our own here. Man has free will. Women, too. And chickens.

"I could throw the I-Ching. Or just toss any coin, heads or tails. What do you think I should do, Tony?" Chick was desperate for another opinion.

"Whoa, I don't want to get involved," Tony held up his hands, palms out. "Whatever you decide, I'll drive you where you need to go. Not all the way to Mexico," he said with a laugh.

In the pre-dawn hours of a sleepless night spent arguing with herself, her demons, and her guardian angels, Chick finally came to a decision. She would trust in the universe and have faith that everything is unfolding as it should. She would fly to Tucson and take a bus from there into Mexico.

20

South Of The Border

"How can I ever repay you for all your kindness?" Chick asked Tony as they left the house at 4:00 a.m. for her early morning flight. "Come to Two-Lip and I'll make it up to you. I'm not much of a cook but I make a mean salad, a meal in itself. And thanks for trying to teach me to play the banjo. I tried. I loved hearing you play. You're wonderful. You sound like Earl Scruggs."

Cutting it close once again, Chick dashed through the airport, arriving at her gate just as they called for final boarding. The flight took her from San Antonio to Salt Lake City to Tucson, a path that made sense only to the airline. Chick was thrilled to see snow on the ground in Utah, although no one else seemed to be.

"I haven't seen snow in twenty-five years," she excitedly told her seatmate.

"I have," said the man ruefully.

Once in Tucson she had all day to do . . . what? She was low on funds until the first of the month. Now if I were here with Teda, it would be a different story, reminisced

Chick with a sad sigh. She had never heard a word from the bird again.

She was a resourceful chicken. For just one dollar round trip she climbed aboard a city bus, rolling her luggage behind her. Half an hour later, she disembarked in the arts district, a rather seedy looking area. The only place open for a bite to eat was a dive bar with limited fare or a fancy looking restaurant she deemed above her budget. Chick chose the bar, and was pleasantly surprised to see a veggie burger on the menu. Overall the jaunt was a disappointment, as the few art galleries around were closed, but it was better than sitting in the airport, or the bus station. She had apparently read the map wrong. The Tufesa bus station was nowhere near the airport. She was forced to take a taxi. Eighteen dollars with the tip. Yikes. Big bucks for the chicken!

I'm nervous, she admitted to herself as she entered the station. Most, if not all of her friends were aghast that she would venture solo by bus to a part of Mexico new to her. Alamos was not San Miguel, a popular destination full of tourists. But Chick was convinced the threat of violence was overdone. She would be careful, not walk alone after dark (remembering her last encounter) and not travel through drug infested areas. She had once read the warnings other countries gave to their citizens about travel to the US. Her own country didn't sound like a safe place at all, especially for females.

An hour later she was on the bus, seated right behind the driver, shivering. It was a first class bus and luxurious, but she was freezing. When they stopped in Nogales, Chick went into her luggage and put on nearly all the clothes she had with her, looking silly but feeling warm. The checkpoint below the border had been no problem due to Chick having met and teamed up with a pretty young Canadian woman. Assuming they were together, the agent cheerfully stamped both their visas for the maximum stay of one hundred eighty days, leering and grinning at the attractive blonde. They both got a green light which meant no search of their luggage. Being searched could cause you to be detained and miss your bus, causing no end of hassle.

Hurtling through the darkness, Chick slept in fits and starts, swapping stories with the Canadian woman, who always seemed to be wide awake. She shared her chocolate bar with a Mexican man across the aisle. Eight hours later she and Vanessa said their goodbyes in the town of Navajoa and Chick disembarked. It was still dark. The bus station, the wrong one, as she soon found out, was thankfully open and brightly lit. After walking in the early dawn for two blocks in the wrong direction, she vowed to become proficient in Spanish. With minutes to spare, she found the old station and the Albatros bus that would take her the fifty miles to Alamos. The bus was nearly ready to leave. It's all part of the adventure, thought Chick as she boarded the rickety vehicle, a crowded second or third class bus with a cracked windshield and broken seats. Squeezed in next to the grimy window, she tried to stay awake to no avail.

Awakened by a knocking on the glass, the chicken squinted sleepily at the faces of her old friends, looking . . . older. Had it really been seven years since they'd seen each other? As they trudged up the steep hill to their casita, the pals got reacquainted.

"We love it here. The United States is like a looney bin. Work. Shop. Drive. Work. All as fast as you can. It's laid back here in Alamos," Aaron told her. "Our living costs are a fraction of what they were in the States. We can create our line of jewelry at a relaxed pace, when we're ready, book a show in Tucson and return with a pocket full of cash."

And it was just a sleepy little town. There were only a handful of shops, two art galleries, an upscale hotel with a picturesque restaurant and a museum. Whatever will I do here? The question popped into Chick's head. Aaron and Emilio had told her it was like San Miguel fifty years ago. She hadn't quite grasped the meaning of that until now. What it meant was . . . no colorful crowds, no dancing, no festive strolling on the jardin, not much for the tourist in search of adventure. As she would soon discover, a big pastime for the local gringos was getting together for dinner and drinks and gossiping about the other gringos. At one of these dinners hosted by a high-powered lawyer from Phoenix, she heard Alamos compared to the old TV show, Gilligan's Island.

"You've got a group of people thrown together in a small space and forced to associate with one another," said Larry. "The language barrier isolates us." It was true, the majority of expats in town spoke little Spanish. Of her old pals, Aaron was quite fluent. Emilio, although of Hispanic heritage, could barely say hola y adios.

When Aaron's son from Pennsylvania showed up unexpectedly, Chick had to sleep on the futon in the living room. He was half Chick's age, but he suffered from a variety of ailments, a bad back among them. This arrangement wouldn't have bothered her except for the dogs, one of whom had prior claims on the couch. The sweet old dog had arthritis and moved painfully, but Chick had to sleep somewhere. Coaxing Duchess off the futon and down to the floor was a nightly ritual.

A week later Chick was beginning to feel restless as the days dragged on. The guys spent a good part of the afternoons stockpiling their beautiful jewelry. Buddy had a stack of books he was intent on reading. She hadn't brought any art supplies and there was nowhere to buy them in this town. Even grocery shopping was a welcome diversion. When Aaron suggested a trip to the beach, Chick gratefully agreed.

Playa Huatabampito, a tiny coastal village on the sea of Cortes was virtually deserted. They were the only customers for lunch at the lovely eatery directly on the sand, the colorful tables set gaily for non-existent customers. The adjacent RV park was totally empty. A failing economy and fear kept American tourists from vacationing in this out of the way spot. Still, the food seemed fresh and tasted delicious. Buddy ordered ceviche, the seafood looking not quite dead. Chick could barely watch him eat it. They left a big tip. The economic situation was disastrous for the locals who had depended on the foreign dollar. Sadly, it was the same way in Alamos. Even the luxury hotel was struggling.

At the nearby fishing pier, as they climbed out of their big shiny pickup, the fisherman stared at them blankly. Chick felt like the ugly American, even more so as Buddy carried on a loud conversation on his cell phone about collecting rent at his properties in Philly, of all things. An old woman hobbled over in the hope of selling some trinkets and hand woven bracelets, a shy little girl hiding behind her skirts. The children all seemed to have beautiful shining black hair and dazzling white teeth, despite the meager surroundings. Chick bought a beaded necklace, Aaron, an array of milagros. A pittance in the face of so much need.

Happily for the little chicken, who was in danger of being bored to death, things changed for the better. In the next week, Alamos and Ms. Little underwent a radical transformation. How had she missed the posters around town? Had Aaron told her and she'd simply forgotten? Thursday marked the start of the FOAT Music Festival, named for the famed opera singer, Alfonso Ortiz Tirado, who was born in Alamos. Overnight, the town was teeming with tourists, musicians clustered on the corners making music of all kinds, singers belted out tunes in the public halls, traditional dancers whirled about on an enormous stage in the Plaza. Impromptu mariachi bands strolled, gathering in the streets and parks. Chick made a new friend, Esther, one of those gregarious individuals who knew everyone, who lit up a room with her smile, and was involved in anything of importance in the community. She was married to Lorenzo, a Mexican man who was a lifelong resident of Alamos. Also an artist, Esther was known for her larger than life pastel portraits, capturing with perfection, the quirky faces of the local characters.

"You could run for Mayor, E," joked Chick, as they sat on the patio of the Hacienda.

"I'm thinking about it, es mi sueno." She spoke perfect Spanish and had a bevy of Mexican friends. The day before, she had taken Chick out to the tiny village of La Uvalama to bring supplies to a woman she was close to. Rural families like this one cooked outside on wood stoves, summer and winter. Just as in San Miguel, the contrast with the gringos who lived in mansions overlooking Alamos, who hosted lavish parties and wore designer clothes was astounding. Chick pondered once again the unjust ways of this world. The ever-widening gap between the haves and the have-nots was distressing. She was aware that she herself would be considered rich by Marta, whose humble home they had just left. The running water came through a hose from a shared well. Five people lived and slept in two small rooms, a child in a wheelchair sat in the dirt yard.

Stretched out on the futon that evening, her inner dialogue kept Chick wide awake. Who am I to point fingers at the rich? In Mexico, I'm viewed as a privileged and affluent individual with my house and my new car, my ability to jump on a plane and travel where I like. I could be using my money to help others like Marta and her family instead of gallivanting around the country. But I don't live extravagantly, she argued with herself. It's not as though I have buckets of money to give away. And now that I'm not working anymore . . . I do help out when I can.

Chick slept fitfully that night, for deep in her heart, she knew she was only rationalizing her own selfish behavior.

21

Ms. Fortune

Huffing and puffing like the big bad wolf, Chick flopped down on a bench to catch her breath. She and Buddy had hiked to the top of the Mirador. Alamos in miniature spread out before them in adobe colors and blinding whites. The mountains were a deep violet, the sunlit patches, magenta and salmon pink. They could glimpse a corner of Aaron and Emilio's casita and the humongous green arches welcoming one into town. Many deemed these odd structures a useless project along with the hundred or so street lights that no longer worked. This expenditure could have helped to fund a modern water system, something the town was sorely in need of. The wheels of bureaucracy turn slowly in Latin America. Like the US, a lot of folks had their hands in the pot.

The view the two had won by the tiring climb was spectacular. Chick was happy to get some vigorous exercise. Unfortunately, she found getting down was far worse than the climb up, descending the seemingly endless steep staircase on shaky legs, muttering under her breath about

the vagaries of getting older. Finally, to her utter mortifi-
cation, Buddy swept Chick up and sat her on his shoulder.

"Quit your complaining, old timer!" he admonished,
laughing. Always direct and abrasive, nonetheless, she liked
him, although he was nothing like his father, Aaron, who
was gentle and soft spoken, a liberal and a true lover of
animals. Much like Chick's own daughter, the offspring
was as different from the parent as night and day.

That evening her hosts threw an elaborate dinner party
at the house. A delicious spread, all vegan, prepared by
Emilio, a former chef. Still, she would bet that the guests
would be unhappy to learn that the dogs were allowed
to lick the plates clean. Chick would keep her lip zipped.

After a healthy toke on a huge spliff offered by one of
the Mexican dinner guests, the party drifted in a purplish
haze down to the plaza for a much anticipated performance
by Alejandra Robles. Energetic and lively, the Afro-Mex
singer belted out tunes everyone wanted to dance to. People moved up to the floor in front of the stage and Chick
followed along with them.

This is when our formerly charmed chicken ran into a
spot of misfortune. One minute Chick was having such
fun dancing, swinging her hips, flailing her wings about,
whirling around, the belle of the ball . . . the next minute she
was suddenly on the ground, flat on her back, stunned and
wondering what had happened. Thank goodness, Buddy
had seen her fall and came running to her aid.

"Stand back! Give her some air!" he told the gathering
crowd in a commanding voice.

"Don't move her," she heard someone say. "Is that a
chicken?" murmured another voice. How embarrassing,
how mortifying, she had enough presence of mind to think.
I will not cry, she told herself, as a sea of concerned faces
peered down at her. Chick knew she was injured. She could
feel pain in her wing, a lot of pain, and as Buddy helped

her to stand, her leg crumpled beneath her. A trickle of blood from a cut on her knee ran into her shoe.

"I'm okay. I'm alright. Please don't make such a fuss," our dear little chicken said bravely. "So sorry to put such a damper on the evening."

"Don't be silly," Aaron said as they all took turns carrying her up the hill to the house. "I fell down just the other day."

"But not in front of five hundred people," answered Chick, choking back tears. In the kitchen of the casita, Buddy sat her on the wooden table and gently cleaned off her scrapes, which didn't appear serious.

"I . . . I can't move my wing," said Chick. And then she did cry.

"I'll put in a call to Esther." Aaron picked up the phone. "She'll know what to do." Of course she would, because Esther knew everything. The whole town of Alamos benefited from her expertise. If she couldn't fix the problem, Esther would know someone who could.

"Half an hour of heat, half an hour of ice, ibuprofen if you have it. Call me back in the morning. If she still has no mobility, I'll bring Elana over to check her out." Elana, a close friend of Esther, was a doctor doing her residency at the local clinic, closed now for the weekend.

In the morning, Chick knew she had overreacted. Buddy, bless his heart, had given her his bed for the night and slept on the futon. He brought her breakfast in bed, on a tray with coffee and a vase of wildflowers. Fully awake, she was able to gingerly move her wing. It hurt. It hurt a lot. On a scale of one to ten, it was a seven, maybe an eight. Not a break, but a bad bruise, they all agreed.

"Take a toke of yerba, mamacita. That will take your pain away." Juan, a guest from the dinner party, had stopped to ask about her. Chick took a hit, laid back on the flowered pillow and slept most of the day, pampered by her dear friends.

The remainder of her stay in Alamos passed slowly, the days blending together in a blur. She went out, to the museum, for short walks, to another concert, where she sensibly stayed seated. Still in pain, she wore a sling Emilio had fashioned for her out of a scarf. Unwisely, she was downing painkillers like candy. One could buy nearly anything here without a prescription. Vicodin, oxycodone. percocet, the whole gamut. Luckily she didn't have an addictive personality. And she didn't like the fuzzy way the drugs made her feel, even though they took the hurting away.

Chick was more than ready to go home, if not to Two-Lip, at least to the States. But could she handle her suitcase and bags with one wing still out of commission? The high-powered lawyer offered her a ride.

"I can get you to Tucson muy pronto," he bragged. "Six hours tops." Chick declined, picturing the gleaming silver Mercedes hurtling through the darkness, causing havoc for pedestrians and wildlife alike. She wanted to survive the trip.

Much to her surprise, Aaron and Buddy decided to return to New Mexico on the next Wednesday by bus. Emilio would close up the house and drive up next week with the dogs. Chick would have to stay for another six days, but have excellent company and help on her return trip. The three planned to take an Express bus, then catch Amtrak in Tucson. She was delighted, her problem solved. The chicken hadn't been on a train in years.

On the morning of the intended departure another near tragedy struck. All packed and ready, but still asleep, the bell on the fence awakened the household in the pre-dawn light. There stood Juan holding a bleeding dog in his arms. It was Manches, one of the street dogs Aaron had been feeding. Now, instead of driving to the bus station, they were making their way thirty miles to the closest animal hospital, the poor dog oozing blood from a wound in his side. What had happened? Had he been hit by a car?

"No, this wasn't an accident," said the vet in Navajo as she stitched him up. "It looks like he was stabbed with a knife. It could be barbed wire, but I don't think so. It's too clean of a cut."

Who would do such a cruel thing and why, they all wondered. "He'll recover," said the vet, "But he needs to remain quiet and the wound kept clean."

It wasn't safe or advisable to put poor Manches back out on the street. All the plans would have to change. Aaron decided to stay behind with Emilio until the dog was well enough to travel. Even though they had their hands full now, the two would adopt him, bringing the sweet dog back to the States. These compassionate men, lifelong vegetarians, loved dogs and all four legged creatures. Chick was proud to call them her friends

New arrangements were made and the tickets changed. The following evening it was only she and Buddy taking the funky old bus to Navajo and then catching the first class bus into Tucson. Her wing still aching, Chick had hoped to sleep through the night with the help of pharmaceuticals and wake up refreshed back in the USA. The bus driver had other plans. Schedules and rules can change in Mexico and frequently do. There were only three other passengers on the Express bus. No one wanted to get off, or apparently get on. The bus sped right by the dimly lit little towns at top speed, arriving at the border in six hours, undoubtedly a record for a Tufesa bus. I may as well have ridden with the lawyer, thought Chick. Speeding seemed to be de rigueur in this part of Mexico.

The 'No Produce' rule at the inspection point of US Customs had completely slipped the chicken's mind. Her bag of avocados and half a dozen oranges in her backpack caused the border patrol agent to froth at the mouth.

"What is this?" the guy snarled, holding up the fruit like they were hand grenades.

"Sorry," said Chick, feeling foolish once again. "I forgot." The agent tossed the bag in the trash. "You could have at least had them for breakfast. They're quite tasty," She looked wistfully at the garbage bin. The man turned around just in time to catch Buddy taking a picture of the exchange.

"No cameras! Can't you two read? I could detain you," the agent said angrily.

"But is it worth it?" laughed Buddy, grinning. "I'm a lawyer." He most certainly was not.

"You come through here again, I'm going to remember your faces. Especially the chicken!" The man glared as he waved them on. Buddy thought the incident hilarious. I wish I could be like that, Chick said to herself. He has no fear. She felt intimidated by the encounter, if not scared. I'm such a chicken, she thought. That she was. A chicken, that is.

The bus had been fast. So fast that she and Buddy found themselves on the deserted streets of Tucson at 3:00 a.m. with nowhere to go, pulling their luggage behind them. The taxi from the bus station had deposited them in front of the Amtrak station, but the doors were shut tight and locked.

"We're sitting ducks. Chickens, I mean," joked Buddy. "But seriously, I've got a pocket full of cash. We need to find some shelter and fast."

A neon sign flashed brightly down the block ahead. The Hotel Jolly.

Once inside, a desk clerk eyed them from behind a caged counter. "We need a room for a couple of hours," began Buddy.

The weasel faced clerk pulled himself up to his full five foot six inch height. "This isn't that kind of place," he said with a smirk, leering at Chick. "And we don't allow farm animals."

"Whoa, mister! You've got this all wrong. My friend

and I have a train to catch at 9:00 a.m. Now, how much for a room?" Buddy said in his nicest voice.

"Let me see if I have anything that would accommodate you. The both of you," sneered the clerk, looking at a computer.

"Yes, I do have one room available. With the taxes, it would be two hundred seventy-five dollars."

"Are you kidding me? This place is a dive!" snapped Buddy.

"The price includes a pet deposit. Two hundred dollars, non-refundable," said the nasty little man.

"Come on, Chick," Buddy grabbed her by her good wing. "Let's get out of here before I do something I might regret."

Back on the street, Chick was mortified. She'd not experienced that level of speciesism in a long time. Was she living in a bubble? Had she just been lucky? Living in la-la land with blinders on? As time passed, Chick would find that she had indeed been lulled into complacency. The disastrous election that would propel another vile man into power, would bring people like the desk clerk out from under their rock, embolden them to spew their hate publicly, was still years away.

"Well, I'd say that place was anything but jolly," said Buddy, glancing back at the hotel's cheery sign.

The two walked in the direction of bright lights. Chick's wing was killing her again. So this is what chronic pain feels like, she moaned under her breath. It wears you down. It makes you cranky. Exhausted, she pressed on.

There! Thank the goddess! Up ahead, a twenty-four hour cafe. Inside it was warm and dry, with loud music and a cast of colorful folks clad in black clothes and sporting lots of metal and piercings. People played a game of darts, most were glued to their cell phones, or bent over laptops. Manga style paintings graced the dark walls.

"Cool! A chicken." A young man with a wide toothy smile nodded to them as they took a seat in a comfortable booth.

The waitress, a sweet looking girl with a pierced tongue and safety pins holding her t-shirt together, took their order, bringing two generous slices of pecan pie and strong hot coffee.

"You look bad!" she told Chick. "I'll bet you got your jacket and backpack in Mexico. Super bad."

Chick knew this statement was meant as a compliment. The two felt welcome in this little hole in the wall. A good thing. They had four hours to kill.

22

This Train

This train wasn't bound for glory. It was bound for New Orleans. In anticipation of Mardi-Gras fun, folks were loud, boisterous, excited and a bit drunk. Buddy was only too happy to exit the train four hours later in Deming, New Mexico.

"You're my knight in shining armor. You saved my butt more than once," Chick thanked him profusely. "Love you, Buddy," she mouthed, waving through the window as he headed away into town. She would miss him, yes, but now she had both seats to herself, two pillows and a shawl she'd bought in Alamos for a blanket. Just as she'd gotten comfortable, the man behind her began loudly complaining to his companion. Chick had heard the conductor call the man to come downstairs at the last stop. It seems the drug sniffing canines had pointed a nose at his bag, the agents ripped it open, breaking the lock and zipper. They found nothing. The man was outraged and let everyone know ad infinitum. Glad it wasn't me, floated through her mind as she dozed off.

Chick was running as fast as her short little legs could carry her. "Wait! Wait for me!" she wailed, as the train disappeared in the distance. "Oh, dear. Why ever did I get off? Oh, yes, I saw a woman selling burritos. But I was only gone for a few minutes!"

A myriad of vendors sold cotton candy, buttered popcorn, hot dogs and fried Twinkies. Costumed dancers cavorted on the platform wearing elaborate masks bedecked in bright feathers and sequins. Freakish figures on stilts towered above her. Is this El Paso? thought Chick. Didn't the conductor say El Paso? Am I in New Orleans? Did I miss my stop? Whatever will I do? Thoroughly confused, the chicken wandered among the crowds, wondering where she was.

Suddenly, the feathers on the back of her neck stood up. The little chicken had the eerie feeling she was being followed. Turning around, she saw a hulking form behind her dressed in flowing robes of black and gold, a big sign hanging from its monstrous shoulders. Squinting in the semi-darkness, she could just make out the words. It read . . . 'Fried Chicken $5.95.' Fear clutched at her heart and she stood frozen in her tracks. A scrawny claw with fierce talons reached out toward her.

"Awk! Awk! Help me! Somebody, please help me!" screamed our feathered friend.

Chick sat bolt upright in her seat, wide awake, stomach churning, sweating, all twisted up in her shawl, her wing throbbing. Another nightmare. She simply should not have eaten that spicy food from the canteen. And one taco would have been plenty, not three. The gooey chocolate bar rounding out the meal was quite over the top. This is what I deserve for stuffing myself. It's my own fault. From now on, I'll stick to fresh fruits and veggies, beans and rice, and not so much of it. Healthy fare. And one glass of red wine. It would be a big glass.

Her train pulled into the San Antonio station right on time, unusual for Amtrak. As she retrieved her suitcase, Chick felt woozy and light-headed. Her beak was stuffed up. It was either the stale air on the train or she was coming down with something.

There stood Tony on the platform, waiting faithfully. What a sweet guy he was. As she climbed into his truck, she sneezed four times.

"So sorry." Sneezing again, she realized she felt terrible, aching all over and though she rarely got headaches, she had one now. Please don't let it be the flu, she said silently. A day later, curled up in the bedroom loft of Tony's cabin, she knew it was only a bad cold and not a flu. But that afternoon an email came in from Aaron, telling her he was down with bacterial pneumonia and that it was contagious. Listening to her body, the chicken was convinced her ailment was a simple garden variety cold, still she stayed upstairs far away from Tony. Chick was loath to visit a doctor, both from a basic distrust and the fact that medical doctors who would treat a domestic fowl were few and far between. She'd been insulted in the past when she was referred to a veterinarian.

Fearful of the possibility of exposing Tony any further (although the damage had probably already been done) and feeling better, she packed her bags, intending to head for a state park just outside of Austin.

"Thank you so much for putting up with me, Tony. Stay well," Chick said from the car window. "Let me know how you're doing, please." She blew him a kiss and drove out through the smoke trees that lined the driveway toward the highway.

Willie Nelson crooned on the radio as she sped down the two lane road. "I'll snuggle up in the car until I feel one hundred percent okay," she said to Willie. "Good girl, Fancy!" she told the car, patting the dashboard. It felt wonderful to be back on her own four wheels. A look at the weather report warned that temperatures were plummeting to the low forties tonight. The state park would have electric hookups. Luckily, Chick had her heater. Hopefully this time she could get it working.

23

The Winter Of Her Discontent

"Oh, for heaven's sake. I'm not sick." Chick said to the nearby tree. She'd been camping solo at McKinney Falls for a week and had no close contact with anyone. Her wing felt fine and she no longer had even a sniffle. Life was good. She loved being on the road, loved being in nature, her feet in the dirt, yet she was feeling the pull of Two-Lip and her own bed.

"Please do come out and have dinner with me, Hope. I'm getting antsy for some company," she told her friend. "Could you grab some food for us? I'll pay. I know I'm asking you to dinner, but I can't stand my own cooking another day," pleaded Chick.

Evening found the two pals munching on vegetarian tamales, a rare treat Hope had found at a food truck in Austin. "I think it's time to go home," Chick said wistfully. as they huddled close to a vintage lamp Hope had pulled out of her car. Plugged into electricity, it gave off a warm glow in the forest.

"I thought you'd have a fire," said Hope unhappily.

"I thought you'd bring firewood," Chick countered. People could be such a disappointment. The Park Service levied a big fine if you burned downed branches, destroying habitat for wildlife, an ecological no-no. Chick had been collecting twigs and small pieces of wood when fortunately, she noticed the warning sign.

Tom Turkey had declined to visit, although he lived only a few miles away. Intuition told her he wasn't much of a caregiver and more than a bit paranoid about catching her 'bug'. Chick didn't blame him. Her time with him in Austin already felt like a dream.

"It was just a casual fling for both of us," she told Hope.

"Aren't they all?" Hope had experienced more than her share of sour encounters with the opposite sex. "That smoky chatter in the dead of night doesn't mean a thing in the harsh light of day, especially with guys named Tom," Hope said bitterly. "I'm done for a while, a long while. Every guy I've met online just wants to hook up on the first date. I'm hoping for a little old-fashioned romance. Flowers and candle-light, the whole bit. Not going to hold my breath," she laughed.

Hope would remain single well into her sixties, when she met and married a wonderful man who, ironically, was named Tom.

"Bye-bye, girlfriend. Traveling mercies," Hope waved to Chick as she drove through the dark toward the exit. As always, any farewell brought tears to Chick's eyes. Tomorrow is not promised. Who knows if she'd ever see the loved one again? She was a sentimental bird.

Having barely slept a wink, the traveler hit the road at first light. Sleepless nights were becoming all too frequent. When did she develop insomnia? Maybe dropping out her afternoon coffee would help. Alas, now she would feel tired today instead of alert. To keep herself awake, the bird snacked on nuts and blue corn chips. Ducky was right, all the crunching made it impossible to doze off while driving.

Texas was big, too big, but finally, there was the 'Welcome To Louisiana' sign. A look at her roadmap told her she could sleep at the same state park she'd camped in on the trip west. So much for new adventures, she thought, but she was too tired to push on. Her old campsite was free, right next to the 'Beware Of Alligators' sign. The night water jug came in handy, as she didn't dare venture out until dawn.

Sipping her morning coffee, she reflected again on the about face her life had taken. Driving still seemed like an utter luxury. If only it had happened sooner. She was truly filled with gratitude that it had happened at all.

Easy peasy, don't you know, I'm just a poor girl on the go. Chick sang along with Queen, making up her own lyrics. Her life was easy, thank the goddess. She'd never killed anyone, never pointed a gun at any living creature, never been in jail. She'd never even owned a firearm and had no plans to, in spite of all the people who told her a gun was a necessity for a female on the road alone.

"Anybody tries to mess with me, I'll just spray them into submission," she joked. She carried an arsenal of sprays, bear spray, three cans of pepper spray, wasp and hornet spray. As yet, she'd never had occasion to use any of it.

Chick crossed the Florida state line some six hundred miles later. Exhausted and grimy, she decided to treat herself to a night at a motel. I deserve it, she told herself. If age sixty-five was considered elderly, then right there was a reason she ought not deny herself a night of clean sheets, fluffy pillows, and a hot shower. With so many downsides, old age should come with a few benefits. Ten or fifteen percent off a meal didn't seem like enough of a reward.

Late the next afternoon, Chick pulled into her driveway, so glad to see her own house, she burst out crying. "Here I am. It's me. I'm home, house!" The house said nothing, but it gave off a welcoming vibe she could feel in her bones.

Soon, she was sitting on her porch, feet up and drinking an icy cold beer, looking out at the lake, very happy to be there. In a few short days it was as if she'd never left. Her big adventures were behind her. In another few weeks, reality set in. Too much was never enough for the little chicken. Was she a perennially discontented soul? She knew that the answer to all life's questions lies within. But self-discipline was not her forte, at least at this point in her life. She couldn't even sit still for twenty minutes of meditation.

"There must be more to life than this," Chick said loudly, forgetting her vow to be grateful for her riches, to content with what she had and where she was. No one had called or stopped by since the first week after her return. In her mind it seemed like an eternity. If I lived in downtown Two-Lip, things would be different, wouldn't they? Six miles out of town may as well have been a hundred miles. Had she already tired of driving into town? Had she forgotten the days when she had to ask for help just to go anywhere? No, no, but her empty feeling persisted. Our sweet little chicken had no inkling that in a matter of days, her life was about to take a radical turn.

24

Ride Like The Wind

Chick swung her tiny SmarterCar into the grassy lot of the Two-Lip Farmers Market, parking next to a man polishing his already gleaming motorcycle. Yum! He looks just like Marlon Brando in The Wild One, thought Chick. Yes, she was still attracted to bad boys.

"What a beautiful bike. It shines like the sun!" she exclaimed. "Are you going to Bike Week?"

"I sure am and I'm looking for someone to go with me," said the handsome guy, a twinkle in his blue eyes.

Chick had seen the biker around town and hanging out at Cavallini's, but never been introduced.

"I'll go," Chick answered impulsively.

"Oh, you will, huh? Are you sure about that? Let's go for a ride right now. See how you like riding. My name's Owen, by the way," said the man, giving her a big smile. Before she knew it, there she was perched on the seat behind him, feathers flying, going eighty on the interstate, no helmet, no seat belt, no worries.

I am one crazy lady, she said to herself when they were

off the motorcycle, having a beer at the Harley-Davidson shop in Gainesville. It was bike night and the parking lot was jammed. Owen's bike wasn't a Harley, it was a Kawasaki. He hated Harleys. Hardly-a-Davidson, he said to her, not within earshot of his die hard Harley pals.

The chicken was more than ready for a stimulating escapade. Come Tuesday, Ms. Little and her new man were off to Daytona. Chick was as excited as a five year old. Her friend, Junie, had given her a pair of high black boots, and someone else, a black leather jacket with fringe. I didn't buy it new, she rationalized, well aware that the cheap leather from China was probably dog. Owen had an extra helmet that fit her perfectly.

"You could lose all your head feathers in the wind. We don't want to see you bald," he said, giving her a big kiss, and strapping on the new yellow helmet securely.

Daytona! Never had Chick seen so many motorcycles in her life. Every color from cherry red to iridescent rainbow flake, every make from Valkyrie to Indian, all shining and blinding chrome, the most prized possession of their proud owner.

"I'll be famous, the first chicken on a bike touring the country, promoting species rights," she told Owen. "I'll get a trike and pull a trailer and . . . " There was our chicken, off on another creative tangent, a habit she had throughout her life. The years were flying by with increasing speed, but she had yet to zero in on one consuming project. Now here she was chasing her dreams from the back of a motorcycle. 'Reflections In A Helmet' would be the perfect title for my memoir, she mused.

Bike Week did not disappoint in the least. It was theater. One could only see such a wild display of individualism as high camp. Long beards, oily blue jeans, sleeveless black vests covered with patches, bare arms displayed a multitude of tattoos. Hells Angels, Support Eighty-One stood out.

Some of these guys were downright scary as they gazed at Chick from afar, their heavy boots and chains intimidating. But she knew that many of the other riders were weekend warriors. Come Monday, they'd clean up and be back at work, an investment banker or a lawyer. And then, there were the lady bikers. Most women rode bitch, like Chick, a passenger on the back. But there were a fair number of women with their own bikes, strong and independent. Most of the men she met looked tough, but when she talked to them they were polite and sweet. Not so the one percenters, flying their colors. They were a different breed and she gave them a wide berth.

Friday night found Owen and Chick at the Cabbage Patch, first, to gawk at the midget wrestlers, then dancing far into the night to Owen's favorite band, Big Engine. Chick was thrilled for Owen when he was asked to sit in as a harp player inside with the house band. He was a top-notch musician and could really bend the notes on his harmonica. Chick was impressed beyond words and totally smitten. She danced with uninhibited recklessness in front of the band, peeling off her shirt and tossing it into the crowd, who clapped and whistled. She was a biker chick now!

Goosey was concerned for her. "What do you think you're doing, Chick?" her friend asked as they sat in the Bay having a glass of wine. It was the same back booth where Teda had uttered the words that broke her heart.

"I'm having fun," answered Chick. "Being on the bike is exhilarating, a little scary, but so liberating. I love it. You should try it, Goosey. Owen has a friend I'm sure you'd like. We'd be the fabulous four!"

"Oh, no. No. Not me, thanks. You could get killed or worse yet, maimed for life. Motorcycles are so dangerous. Why, my cousin was . . . "

"Stop, Goosey. I don't want to hear it. Owen is a good

rider. I trust him with my life. And guess what? We're going to Sturgis!" Chick said excitedly.

"Oh, my God. You have lost your mind. All the way to South Dakota? On a motorcycle?"

"Goosey, I'm having the time of my life! I don't want to sit on my porch telling stories about adventures I used to have. I'm still out there having more fun, making memories. We're going up to Tennessee this weekend and ride The Dragon," Chick told her friend, her voice alive with enthusiasm.

"The what?" Goosey was dumbfounded.

"You'll see. I'll send pictures," Chick told her.

True to her word, she did. Back again in their favorite booth at the Bay, Goosey and Henny looked at the phone in horror. Chick had taken a video from her perch on the bike, filming their ride on The Dragon, eleven miles of serpentine road, three hundred eighteen curves running from Deals Gap north along Route One Twenty-nine northwest of Franklin, North Carolina.

"One of the most dangerous roads in America," Goosey read from the online description. And her foolhardy best friend was on it. "Oh, Chick, we've lost you," sighed Goosey, and Henny, too, as they watched the terrifying video again. The next picture Chick sent was of herself and Owen, alive and in one piece, drinking a beer under the Tree Of Shame, an enormous old oak tree completely covered with bike parts from previous riders mishaps.

"At least she survived. This time," said Henny, shaking her head.

Owen lived life on the edge. A trip to South Dakota from north Florida should take four days. The wind at their back, the afternoon of the third day saw the travelers pulling into the Sturgis Bike Fest, the largest, most popular biker rally in the US. It was Daytona on steroids. Their first stop was the Full Throttle Saloon, billed as 'The World's

Biggest Biker Bar.' Owen and Chick rode the zip line across the top of the bar straight into a restaurant, where they scarfed down the pricey and greasy edibles. All their gear was strapped to the bike, tent, bedrolls, two changes of clothes, socks and undies, a few snacks. Storage space was minimal, packing a challenge. They set up camp at the Days End Campground, a quieter and less expensive option than the famous Buffalo Chip.

The magical days were filled with fun, laughs, dancing and loving, until one evening on the Sturgis midway, Chick, showing off, impulsively picked up a sledgehammer trying to Hit-A-Gong and win a prize. Instantly, an all too familiar sharp piercing pain shot through her body. The chicken had thrown her back 'out'. She limped away from the bright lights, crooked and bent over unnaturally, embarrassed to have Owen see her so vulnerable. In a matter of minutes, she had gone from being the fun girl, to being a burden.

Thankfully, Owen was kind and understanding, having had back problems himself, but Chick was determined to carry on as if nothing had happened. She refused to give up and just lay down. They found a back brace at a thrift store, and, trussed up, she was able to stand straight and climb back on the bike. The two rode to all the famous landmarks, out to Wall Drug, the Eye Of The Needle, Mount Rushmore, Devil's Tower, but Chick saw it all through a haze of pain. Unlike Mexico, it was not so easy to get pharmaceuticals in South Dakota. In desperation, she went to a chiropractor. After a week flat on her back, holed up in a cheap motel, watching television, hitching a daily car ride to the clinic for treatments, the doctor deemed her ready to travel by motorcycle again. And what other choice did she have? She was stranded eighteen hundred miles from home. Still in considerable pain and still wearing the brace, she had to be lifted onto the bike.

Once again, fate was smiling kindly on the unfortunate chicken. Forty miles down the road out of Sturgis, Owen stopped to gas up. He carefully helped her off the bike. Chick was halfway across the pavement on her way to the Mini-Mart, when suddenly the excruciating pain disappeared as quickly as it had come. It was a miracle! She ripped off the brace and stood upright.

"Oh, thank the goddess! I'm okay, Owen. Look at me. I'm fine!" Chick shrieked as she whirled around. And she was fine. Whatever was out of place was now in place. Chick had learned her extremely expensive lesson. Her back, indeed her whole aging body, was vulnerable. Owen was convinced that crawling in and out of the tent and sleeping on the inflatable air mattress was the culprit, the injury not the fault of her lifting the sledgehammer. Wary of a repeat of her infirmity and anxious to get his girlfriend home safely, he insisted they stay in motels on the return trip. Chick had to admit it was far more comfortable. But she much preferred camping under the stars, spending the evening gazing into a campfire. In the middle of Kansas, they were just twenty miles past the World's Largest Ball Of Twine. Owen wouldn't listen to Chick's plea to turn around. In truth, he treated her as if she were made of glass all the way back to Florida.

25

Go West Young Woman

Change comes slowly to little towns like Two-Lip. Indeed, whenever Chick returned from her far-flung journeys, it appeared that time had stood still. She spent more and more of her days out riding with Owen, less time with her old pals, and far less time tooling around in her beloved SmarterCar. The car sat forlornly in her driveway.

Chick knew she was the subject of gossip, a favorite pastime for the inhabitants of any small town, be it in Mexico or Florida, but it didn't bother her. Owen never broke character, he was the quintessential biker and Chick began to look the part as well. Gone were her colorful outfits, flowered skirts and gauzy flowing blouses. It was tight jeans and black tee shirts for this lady biker, a term she loathed.

"I ain't no lady," she declared, if anyone dared to call her that. And yet, a wee bit of doubt about her choice of lifestyle was slowly creeping into her head. Owen was a Bernie supporter and a Democrat, but he was a tiny minority within the biker community. Rubbing elbows with folks who were right-wing, carried guns, and waved flags was wearing on her. Yet, she was no longer interested in peace work or protests, and rarely gave a thought to the leftist politics she had been so involved in. 'No bar too far' was Owen's motto. The couple participated in every local poker run, every bike night, charity run, fall and spring Bike Week in Daytona, rallies from Florida to North Carolina. If there was an event, Owen had to be there. She tried to beg off occasionally but he wouldn't hear of it. He didn't like riding alone. Chick's life had become a blur of thundering pipes, exhaust, black leather, loud music, and beer. Bottles and bottles of beer.

"I don't know anymore if the biker life is really for me," she told Owen late one night. What had seemed so thrilling to her in the beginning, had become repetitive. And though Chick was proud to say she was never bored, this lifestyle had become, to her, exceedingly repetitious, and, yes, boring. But never to Owen. Biker life was always new and exciting to him. Owen lived and breathed all things motorcycle

"Don't bail on me, Chickie," said Owen, giving her a smothering hug and a long soulful kiss. "You're my old lady."

"I am that," she cackled. "It's just . . . I need a change of scenery. What would you say to the idea of a trip to the southwest, just you and me? I barely saw New Mexico or Arizona years ago when I was there. I didn't even see the Grand Canyon. It's one of the Seven Wonders of the World."

Owen looked thoughtful, saying, "I was only a kid when my parents took me on a road trip out west. I don't remember much at all. Except for fighting with my sisters in the back seat. Okay, Chick, let's do it. But if we have to go through Texas and we do, then this time we've got to stop at my sister's place or she'll kill me. And you have to promise to be nice. Look, baby, I was already thinking about buying a cargo trailer to pull behind the bike. We can carry a cooler, a lot more food, chairs, even a hammock. We'll camp in luxury. Glamping, I think it's called." Owen was suddenly full of enthusiasm for the idea.

Much to Chick's delight, before the month was over, the two were on the road heading west. Avoiding I-10, they stayed on the roads less traveled and kept to the blue highways, motoring slowly along the picturesque coastal route through the Florida panhandle, rural Alabama, Mississippi, Louisiana. Finally, they were in Texas, the state that goes on forever and then goes on some more.

Nine hours of riding and Chick's feathered derriere was numb, her nerves frayed. "Are we there yet?" she shouted, sounding like a grumpy child.

"Only another fifty miles. Just chill, doll," Owen yelled back. When, at long last, they arrived at Owen's sister's house, Chick was like a zombie, barely able to speak. A delicious meal was ready and waiting for them. How sweet of her, thought Chick through her brain fog. Afterwards, Luann graciously led Chick to the guest room.

"No sleeping together. You're not married. Sinners in the eyes of God. My house, my rules. Owen gets the couch," said Owen's sister, not unkindly. Chick thought this arrangement quite absurd. They were both over seventy. She could barely stop herself from laughing, but was too polite to say anything contrary in return. The idea of an unseen entity hovering in the sky like a voyeur, watching your every move, was nonsensical to Chick. People are so weird, she said to herself, not for the first time.

Two days later Chick and Owen were standing on the south rim of the Grand Canyon gazing in awe at the incredible beauty spread out before them.

Nearly speechless, Chick said, "It's deep. I had no idea. It's glorious!" This should have been a moment to contemplate the meaning of the universe and one's place in it, to meditate on the nature of self, of life. Throngs of tourists, jostling elbows for a better view, made that next to impossible. Still, the sheer grandeur of the panoramic vista inspired introspection. Her recent stay in an evangelical household had stirred up repressed emotions. Chick had her own moral compass. Christians couldn't agree on whether animals even possessed a soul, and if so, where that soul would end up. In her mind, the nature of the universe was unknowable and unimaginable, the idea of heaven, a fictional slice of pie in the sky. Chick didn't know what happens when one leaves this mortal body, embarking on a journey to the great mystery. And who does? She damn sure knew she had a soul!

There were simply too many people sharing the overlook. The chicken had no wish to ride a donkey to the bottom of the canyon or to hike down into the rocky chasm. Nine hundred people have died at the canyon in a variety of grisly ways. Chick didn't want to add one more being to that grim statistic. She stayed far back from the edge, holding firmly to the guard rails when there were any. She stared at another couple, selfie stick extended, their back to the vast canyon, standing precariously just a few feet from a two hundred foot drop off. People aren't just weird, they're quite insane, she marveled to herself.

The Grand Canyon and the red rocks of Sedona behind them, the pair blew through Phoenix on a Sunday morning heading for Quartzsite, Arizona. Chick was intrigued by all she'd read about the tiny town of two thousand that literally swelled to a million people come January and February. She was not disappointed. Every imaginable recreational vehicle was there, running the gamut from six hundred thousand dollar Class A motorhomes to loners living out of a car and a tent and every rig in between. You could set up camp with a group of like-minded folks or find privacy behind a clump of mesquite. People attempted to claim their spot with elaborate rock gardens delineating their own bit of Bureau Of Land Management (BLM) land. A mere forty dollars for two weeks would get you water, pit toilets, garbage bins, and an RV dump station. Further out of town one could camp for free, just you and the desert, no amenities.

Chick and Owen were newbies. It was all a learning curve. The pair chose a site in La Posa South, paid the meager sum, and set up their tent on the edge of a wash. Too close as they would later learn, when during a rainstorm, the dry wash became a raging torrent, coming within inches of their tent. The setting, under a towering majestic saguaro, Chick's favorite cactus, was walking distance to the primitive bathrooms. Fiery red and brilliant pink sunsets slashed across the sky nightly, turning the prickly cactus to orange, and the distant mountains, a deep purple, the silhouette worthy of a postcard.

Downtown Quartzsite was short on supplies, with only a small grocery store or two, a hardware store, and the ever present dollar stores. People drove north to Parker to shop, or west across the Colorado River into Blythe, California to shop at Smart And Final, an odd name for a grocery store chain, in Chick's opinion. Pizza and beer at Silly Al's with a rock and roll band on the weekend delighted her no end. Every tune had her and Owen up on the dance floor even if no one else danced. It was over a beer at the VFW that another biker told them about the Magic Circle. Unbeknownst to them, a mile or so up the road from their campsite was a clothing optional zone, four hundred fifty acres set aside by the BLM to enjoy nature sans clothes, in the buff, au naturel. Nude!

"The magic people host a Christmas dinner, a New Year's Eve bash, theme dances with a DJ every Friday," Phil told them. "Check it out. Friendly group of folks. This week is pirate night."

Owen winked at Chick. The couple could easily put

together a pirate costume, it being their favorite attire for Halloween back in Two-Lip. A visit to the Salvation Army store supplied what they lacked. It does say clothing optional, thought the chicken, a bit apprehensively. Neither one of them had ever been to a nudist colony, now better known as a naturist camp. A new grand experience!

Friday night saw the pair decked out in all their finery, peering in through the glass door of the Magic Circle dance tent. Everyone was . . . naked.

"I don't know if I'm up for this," said Owen, his voice quavering. "I've never. I just . . . um, I . . . " His voice trailed off. Chick took another look inside. The glass door was quite foggy, but it did appear that the proper attire was . . . nothing.

"Hey, if we don't like it, we'll leave. We don't even know these people," said Chick in an uncharacteristic display of bravery. "Let's go in."

The newcomers were warmly welcomed, big smiles all around. People complimented them on their clever outfits, which they slowly shed, piece by piece until they too were virtually nude. Chick kept her jewelry on, Owen his pirate hat. Bodies come in all shapes and sizes, young or old, she observed. Clothes make the man, it was said long ago. And the woman, too. Pretenses set aside, people behaved naturally for the most part, without artifice. Looking around, Chick saw that few of the revelers were totally naked. Folks wore shoes, cowboy boots, scarves, hats, even a tee shirt or two. Several people were fully clothed. Their biker buddy, Phil, was there with his girlfriend, she being one of the few who were covered head to toe.

"I call him the naked guy," she said affectionately. They did make an odd couple. This relationship won't last, thought Chick, and she was right. The next time they saw Phil, he was single again.

Magic Circle became a hangout for the pair. When

temperatures dropped into the forties, tall propane heaters kept bare bodies warm. Chick and Owen joined the group for a Christmas Day potluck. With the exception of two men, strangely enough, everyone was clothed.

"Maybe it seems sacrilegious," Chick whispered to Owen. Yet the nude men were as welcome as anyone else. Naturists were a non-judgmental crowd. She was the only fowl but didn't feel ostracized in any way.

Unfortunately, the meal was not vegan or vegetarian. Center stage was the ubiquitous turkey and ham. Chick bit her tongue. She was sure there was butter in the mashed potatoes. She ate them anyway.

You haven't lived until you've partied naked on New Year's Eve in the middle of the desert on BLM land, they would tell friends, once back in Two-Lip. How amazing and unexpected to find an oasis of freedom and light, openness and gaiety right there on government land deep in the Arizona desert.

Chick would return. The little chicken was sure of that.

26

A Scary Story

A visit to the state of California was not on the itinerary. While perusing the road atlas, Chick realized just how close the city of Twenty-Nine Palms was to Quartzite, and she was anxious to change the plans.

"I never thought I'd see Charlotte again," she said of her dear friend from Florida. "And now here she is only two hours away. Oh, pretty please, let's do it." pleaded Chick. "We can sleep in a real bed together in Char's guest room and have a shower." The enticing prospect of a hot shower convinced Owen. He had been all set to head east, more than ready to go home.

"If I'm going to California, then I need to see my baby sister in Los Angeles. I can't be in the same state and not visit her. You've got to promise you'll ride with me," Owen told her. Chick readily agreed.

On Saturday afternoon, they stood knocking at the door of Charlotte's house, a cute little adobe with a great view of the Marine Corps training base. The facility was far enough away to look like a fairyland, especially at night, and a stone's throw to the South entrance of Joshua Tree National Park. They had taken Route Sixty-Two, an unbelievably desolate road from Parker, Arizona, straight into Twenty-Nine Palms. The interstate may have been safer, but not a preferred roadway for motorcycle riders. Chick hated the monstrous roadways and shut her eyes when riding through big cities like El Paso and Houston. Equally disconcerting in Chick's mind was a forty mile stretch on their morning ride without seeing another vehicle, but spotting plenty of vultures. She pictured her bones, sun bleached, lying undisturbed in the desert for years. Her heart flew into her throat, when Owen suddenly braked for a jackrabbit crossing in front of them. Maybe the interstate would have been a better choice, after all.

Charlotte was delighted to see them. They were both looking forward to seeing the amazing Joshua trees, but a visit to the park could wait a day or two while Char showed them around her favorite local places. Giant Rock was one of them, possibly the largest free standing boulder in the world. Seven stories high, sadly it was partially covered in graffiti. Some people are clueless morons, they all agreed. In nearby Sanders, they were suitably impressed with the marvel that was Integratron, even if none of them could afford a sound bath. Chick thought she could feel the magnetic energy inside the dome, even from the gift shop.

Lingering over a pancake breakfast, the trio got off to a late start the next morning for a hike in Joshua Tree. Once again, the Golden Age Passport saved them a considerable sum. One of the few perks of aging, it was only ten dollars for a lifetime, a true bargain. That incredible deal would change in the future, but luck was with these three senior citizens.

"Do we all have our water jugs, hats, sunscreen?" asked Charlotte.

"Yes and no," answered Chick. As for sunscreen, Chick

never used it. She was not a fan of slathering her body with unknown chemicals. Anyhow, she had her feathers.

Although they were too early in the season for the cacti to bloom with their amazing and spectacular flowers, the high desert is ever beautiful and fascinating.

"Dozens of species of birds nest in the Joshua trees, innumerable animals feed on the fruits, flowers, and seeds of this unusual tree. Tall, twisty succulents, they are a unique tree and rare in the world," Char read from the brochure. "Aren't I the lucky one to have this treasure at my back door?" She certainly was and Chick was envious.

The friends meandered the twisting trails for hours. Now, it was late afternoon and Chick was feeling tired. Her companions were still full of energy.

"There's plenty of daylight left," said Charlotte. "You can't miss seeing Skull Rock. Very creepy!" Back at the car, they replenished their water bottles and made their way to the trailhead. The Rock wasn't far from the road, just a short walk. Yes, it did resemble a skull, an enormous skull with two blackened eyes. They pressed on far past the Rock, hoping to get up high enough in elevation for a spectacular view of the sunset. Not wanting to be a spoilsport, Chick pushed herself beyond her limits. Eventually, her little legs were ready to give out.

"You don't want to have to carry me back to the car," she jokingly told the two of them. "I'll just sit on this rock right here and rest up. No worries, you go ahead."

"Are you sure, Chick? You don't mind?" Charlotte asked.

"Not in the least. I'll be fine. And I have my phone. Send me a picture from the top." Glancing around for crawling critters, she sat down gratefully on a flat outcropping. Several other hikers greeted her as they went by, heading for the parking area. So late in the day, it was very quiet and peaceful. I wouldn't mind camping here solo, she thought. One did have to stay in a designated campground. You are not truly without company here, unless you ventured out among the rocks for a long hike.

Forty-five minutes had gone by. She was quite alone now. Chick suddenly needed to relieve herself. The delicious lunch of extra spicy burritos had caught up with her. Oh dear, did she have tissues? I'll just go behind this big rock, she thought. But she was still in view of the path. Ever modest, she walked a bit further. Still not far enough. She was reluctant to be caught with her pants down. She'd have to dig a hole. And with what? Oh, why did this have to happen? A perfectly natural function, but at a very inconvenient time. In amongst the boulders she went, searching for the right spot.

At last, there behind that teddy-bear cholla looked private enough. She scraped a hole with a small pointed rock, not nearly the required eight inches, and squatted. What's a chicken to do? Finished with her business, she wadded up the paper and stuck it in her pocket (yuck). Straightening her clothing, Chick set off on the path towards the trail. But where was the path? Quite dim now, dusk you would say, and one direction looked the same as another. It was that way, she said to herself confidently, just past the funny shaped rock. She hurried off to her right. The trail should be just ahead. But it wasn't.

"All right. I'll turn around and go back. The way must have been to the left of that rock, not the right," she mumbled. Now she couldn't find the odd shaped rock. How far had she walked? "No, it's this way. I'm sure I passed under that tree." She walked briskly toward the tallest Joshua tree. The sky was nearly dark, the now unfamiliar tree looked ominous, its branches reaching out toward her like the claws in her nightmares.

"I'm lost," she finally had to admit. "I think I'm lost. Oh, of course. Silly me. My phone. I'll just call Owen." Reassured, she pulled out her phone and tapped in Owen's number. There was no signal. There had been four bars, but now there weren't any.

"Oh, no!" cried the distraught little bird. She felt like a fool, an old fool. What would she do? Snakes and scorpions and spiders all came out at night. The chicken stood rooted to the spot in terror. With a stroke of insight, she remembered her phone was also a flashlight. Finding the setting, she shone the welcome light all around her feet. Light! But what if the battery runs out? Another worry. She played the light up on the rocks and then turned it off, plunging her into total darkness.

Where are they? Are they trying to find me? Did they leave without me? Was this all a calculated plan to get rid of me? Although her rational mind knew the idea was ludicrous, bizarre thoughts crept in.

"Help! Help!" She yelled as loudly as she could. People get lost all the time in Joshua Tree National Park, Chick had read. Some were never seen again. Will anyone ever find me? My bones will look like any bird, the remains of someone's snack, she thought pitifully. She was becoming irrational and panic was setting in. You're not considered a missing person for twenty-four hours. Is that true? No, that doesn't apply to hikers. Or does it? She turned on the flashlight again and began walking, heedless of direction. There was no moonlight to help guide her. Nothing seemed familiar. How could it? The Skull Rock was huge but none of these big rocks was the Skull. The tiny chicken stumbled on, frightened and whimpering.

Just as she'd almost given up hope, her earlier vision on the highway come true, and resigning herself to a tragic death in the desert, she heard voices in the distance.

"Chick! Chick!" Someone was calling her name.

"Here! I'm here!" she squawked, her voice echoing in the rocks. "Oh. Oh, my God, I'm saved." She nearly collapsed with relief as the voices got louder.

"Turn on your phone's flashlight so we can find you. Shine it upright." She recognized Owen's voice.

"There you are!" Owen and Charlotte ran to her, enveloping her in their arms. She was never so glad to see anyone in her whole life.

"Thank goodness you're safe. We were so terribly worried." Half a dozen other people were with them, one a park ranger.

"Another few minutes, and we'd have called in Search and Rescue, Ma'am. You are one lucky lady. Very easy to get confused out here if you leave the trail," he said sternly. Chick didn't feel lucky. She was totally drained. She felt vulnerable and weak.

"Would you please carry me, Owen?" she asked him, all pride having left her. He swept her up in his arms and before long they were safely in the car, driving home, her ordeal at an end. Back in Charlotte's kitchen, Chick ate in silence, not up to talking, She couldn't even smile when the others attempted to make light of the situation. It could happen to anyone, they told her. Barely able to finish her meal, she said an abrupt good night and went to bed.

In the morning she was still in a stupor, thoroughly shaken by last night's events. She'd lost her zip and vigor, her confidence in herself at a low point. Looming ahead of her was a two thousand mile trip on the back of a motorcycle. The logical and most direct route was I-10, a most daunting prospect. Owen still wanted to visit his sister, but he would have to go without her, she told him.

"I'm sorry. I know I promised, but I can't ride into LA. I just can't. Please try to understand," she said. A puzzled look on his face, he agreed, but Chick knew he didn't truly understand. She wasn't sure that she herself understood.

After Owen left, Chick confided in Char. "I think I'm done being a biker chick. I love him, but . . . I'm so tired of being a passenger on the back of that bike. I miss my own car, my independence, my old friends. I've had some wonderful times with Owen, but I feel like it's over."

"Oh, Chick, given the circumstances, it's a bit too early to be done, unless you feel like getting on a Greyhound. He seems like a great guy and he loves you. Get back to Florida first and give it all another think," cautioned her friend.

The motorcycle roared down the highway with Chick once again perched on the pillion of the bike, her mind left to wander as the miles stretched out interminably. Three days gave Chick plenty of time to ruminate. She did not bounce back from the incident at Joshua Tree. She wasn't much fun. In fact she was a tad unpleasant. She was a bitch. A bitch riding bitch..

"I can't seem to do anything right in your eyes anymore," complained Owen with complete justification. The three-day ride felt like three years. When they bypassed New Orleans without even a thought of going into the city, they both knew the relationship was over. It had run its course and died a natural death.

Finally home, safe in her driveway, she dismounted the bike for the last time. Chick felt she had dodged a bullet. Her days as a biker chick had come to an end. It was fun while it lasted.

27

A Great Leap Forward

Chick's days as scooter trash were over. She was home, her feet on solid ground once again. In the early mornings, she sat drinking her coffee on the porch, watching the two resident sandhill cranes walk up to check out the bird feeders. The porch was her favorite part of the house. She'd even turned it into a sleeping place. Last night she heard a screech owl in the massive live oak overhanging the roof. An opossum made his home under the deck, a black snake hung out by the pond, hoping for a breakfast of frogs.

"I live in paradise," she said to the brown and white patterned gecko, sunning itself in a late afternoon patch on the screen. And yet there was something lacking. The chicken couldn't deny the fact that a deep and growing dissatisfaction with her life had set in. A song from the sixties played in her head, Peggy Lee's "Is That All There Is?' A worm she seemed unable to get out of her mind.

Is this it? she asked herself. Will I sit alone on my porch slowly turning into a withered old crone, worrying about hurricanes, a hole in the roof, the AC going out, the septic overflowing, the gutters clogging up? Versions of these dreaded scenarios paraded through her head with alarming frequency. If I fell off a ladder, my remains could lie undiscovered for days or even weeks. When someone calls and you don't answer, they don't think you're dead or injured. No, they think you're not home. Gone camping, off on a trip. She and Dahlia talked only infrequently. Chick was no longer as close with Goosey or Henny or any of her old buddies. And they were all getting older. Sadly, Henny was in the early stages of dementia. Turkey had survived a heart attack. Even in a Blue Zone, one eventually succumbs to various ailments and inevitable death. Chick was feeling quite alone. She was no longer involved with Bananas. Her life had gotten all tangled up with Owen and living the biker lifestyle. And now he was gone too.

"I guess I could find a new boyfriend," Chick told the gecko, but in her heart she knew that wasn't the answer. Know thyself. Was she still, at her advanced age (seventy-five!) still searching for inner wisdom? Still struggling to find her authentic self?

"Who am I?" pondered the chicken. She'd had a lifetime to answer these still elusive questions. Was the answer within or to be found out there somewhere? Or here on her porch? Like Georgia O'Keeffe, she couldn't stop longing for the southwest. The red rocks, the saguaros, the prickly chollas, the vast emptiness of the desert called to her. Her terrifying experience in Joshua Tree had faded to a dim memory. She loved the stark dry wind and the shifting sand dunes, even the tumbleweeds and the dust devils. The desert was the opposite of Florida, with its smothering tropical plant life and strangling vines, the relentless humidity and the overwhelming greenery threatening to overtake everything in its path.

Chick had experienced a tiny taste of the RV life, the freedom from those homeowner worries. She was envious of the full-timers, whose only concerns appeared to be of their rig breaking down. The people she'd met in Quartzite had seemed so carefree. And she remembered meeting Christine on her first trip west, a woman the same age as Chick who'd been living in her RV for over a decade. What an adventurer! The more deeply she thought about it, the more she realized that this was the life she wanted for herself, to live out her remaining years as a free spirit, unencumbered by the responsibility of home ownership. To exchange the security of the familiar for the unknown. The fact that things are not always what they seem didn't cross her mind. Once again our little chicken looked out at the world through rose-colored glasses.

"Am I dreaming? Could I sell my house and live on the road? Could I be a nomad?" she asked of the ever-present gecko on the screen. Could I live in my car? That thought brought her fantasies to an abrupt halt. "Of course I couldn't live in my tiny car." She had rejected the idea of any more long tent camping trips. It was simply too uncomfortable for her old bones. "But I could live in a van. I wonder if Ford makes a SmarterVan? What time is it? I'll just call Santa Fe Ford right now."

It was 7:00p.m. The dealership was closed. She called Goosey but got her machine. No answer at Ducky's either. No matter, they would just try to talk her out of her newest Great Idea, and so would Dahlia. But Chick was already fixated on the possibility of an exciting future.

"I'm not too old to do this," she said to the empty porch, her voice an echo in the dark. The gecko had gone to bed. After a restless night full of dreams of the open road and an early morning nightmare of being chased across the desert by a coyote, Chick awoke feeling even more determined. Promptly at 9:00 a.m., she was on the phone to John out in Alachua.

"Of course I remember you, Chick. You're not easily

forgettable," said the salesman. Unsure of how to take that statement, she pressed on.

"Do you have a van like my car? A SmarterVan for a chicken of my height?" she asked anxiously, holding her breath for his answer, her stomach aflutter. Her whole plan, indeed her whole life, hung on his words.

"Why, yes, Chick. Ford came out with a full size van only this year. Exactly what you're looking for." She gasped out loud and her heart sank when he told her the sticker price. "But I do have a demo here for sale with a few minor issues," he continued. "I can get you into that van for not much more of a payment than you have now. Come on in and take a look."

Chick couldn't get there fast enough. The minute she laid eyes on the van, she knew it was perfect. With the seats removed, it would be gigantic inside, like a house, a home on wheels, she thought, her mind churning out ideas like wildfire. Paperwork completed, new loan approved, she took possession then and there, transferring her things into the new van. To be sure, the van wasn't absolutely perfect. It was a dull shade of hospital green, her most unfavorite color. She'd seen enough green to last her two lifetimes. Maybe she could name her van 'Olive' or 'Olivia'.

An hour later she wheeled into downtown Two-Lip. It was Friday and there was a group of her old friends gathered together at the Farmers Market. Chick drove right up on the grass and blasted the horn.

"Come and see my new home!!" screeched Chick.

Epilogue

Two women and a chicken sat clustered around the dwindling embers of their small campfire, as the setting sun turned the cerulean blue skies of New Mexico into a fiery glow of orange and magenta. The shallow waters of Elephant Butte Lake lapped gently at the distant shoreline.

"You were and still are my inspiration, Chris," said Chick, poking at the fire with a stick. "When I first met you way back in Austin, I thought, if this woman can survive and prosper out here on the road, then so could I. After all, neither one of us is getting any younger," laughed Chick.

"Super happy it's working out for you." Chris gave her a big smile. "I'd be the first to admit I felt apprehensive and even a wee bit guilty. After all, there you were selling your house, uprooting your entire life, leaving behind the comforts of home, with little old me as a role model. Remember, I did tell you it wouldn't be easy. I've been on the road for eleven years. This is my third Toyota Dolphin," Chris chuckled. "Breaking down, finding another rig more than once, it was a real challenge, let me tell you."

"Christine, I would never blame you for a hot minute if this way of life turns out to be not what I wanted. I'm one hundred percent responsible for my own decisions," Chick said emphatically. "And Pat, I'm so happy we've met. I'm beyond impressed with your gorgeous vardo wagon and hearing all about your travels," Chick told the other member of their little group.

"Chick, did you know that Chris here was my major motivation to get out of sticks and bricks and on the road, too? I watched 'Without Bound' over and over again. I knew I had to come face to face with my heroine, and now here we are friends," Pat said warmly. "It took me a year to design and build my vardo. She's tiny, but perfect for me." The wagon, named 'Wandering Rose', was gorgeous, a painted garden of colorful flowers done in Pat's unique style. The tiny house on wheels was an artist's dream. Chick was inspired. She had already bought brushes and a dozen jars of paint, ready to turn her own van into a masterpiece.

"All our rigs are so different, but they're home sweet home to us full-time nomads," said Christine. "Now, me, I'm not an artist. My forte is communication. I love putting people together. We all have a different vision for our life on the road. And you'll find that people hang together because of their rigs. Class A's, class C's, tenters, van-lifers, that would be you, Chick, and my favorite, Toyota motorhomes. I adore my Toyota family! And Chick, I do hope you meet up with my friend, Randy Vining, the poet, out here on the road. He's a fascinating guy and would be an inspiration to you."

"Thanks so much, you two, for all this information. I already love van life. I love my van, 'Olive'. She is green, at least for now," said Chick dreamily. "And I have to make it work. I don't have enough money to buy another house," she said with a snort. "This is my backyard now." She waved at the vast expanse of starlit sky. "They'll have to pry my cold dead wings from the steering wheel." Pat and Chris howled with laughter.

"Go to the RTR next year in January, Chick," Chris said. "The Rubber Tramp Rendezvous. You'll meet amazing people, maybe even talk with Bob Wells. And learn everything you need to know about living this unique lifestyle."

"And more than you need to know about bathroom etiquette," laughed Pat. "Where to, how to, even when to." Poop conversations were a constant and necessary part of nomad life, as Chick was to learn. Seemingly everyone wanted to share how they carried out their most intimate bodily functions.

The new day dawned, a shimmering sunrise over the peaceful lake. The friends all had differing plans. Pat would stay on at Elephant Butte. She'd stumbled upon a hidden and remote circular rock outcropping, still within the Park, that would afford her privacy for the near future, possibly longer. The fourteen day stay limit was up for Chris. She planned to head south to Las Cruces, where she would park in one of her many friends' driveways for a visit and a welcome respite from the road.

And Ms. Chick Little, our intrepid and brave little chicken? Venture north towards Santa Fe? Head west to Silver City? Or further on to the Oregon coast? Her new life spread out before her like a roadmap. Her destiny was in the stars. She was free to wander in any direction she pleased.

Acknowledgments

Many thanks to my early readers for your help and advice: Susan Ward Mickleberry, Annie Hughes, Dakotah Moon, Raje Anand, Chris Carrington, Pat Guerard, my cousins, Monica Wiley and Katie Wiley. And to Andre Pilon, for your unfaltering support, even when I wanted to quit. Thank you.

About the Author

Hannah Ruth Price was raised in the '50s amidst the whimsical chaos of an Ohio amusement park.

A full-time nomadic artist, illustrator, and poet, she draws her inspiration from the vibrant tapestry of the flora and fauna of the desert Southwest.

Her artwork is cherished by collectors and is in the permanent collection of the Marietta Museum of Art and Whimsy and the International Showmen's Museum.

Email Hannah at kitfox789@gmail.com, and follow her on Instagram: instagram.com/kitfox789.

Made in United States
Troutdale, OR
10/05/2024

23440211R00105